Rosemary's Retribution

Nandita Chakraborty

First published by Busybird Publishing 2018

ISBN
Print: 978-1-925692-99-0
Ebook: 978-1-925692-52-5

Cover image: Kev Howlett
Cover: Kev Howlett
Author Photo: Kev Howlett
Cover design: Busybird Publishing
Layout and typesetting: Busybird Publishing
Editor: Beau Hillier

Busybird Publishing
2/118 Para Road
Montmorency, Victoria
Australia 3094
www.busybird.com.au

For Belinda and Rajvi

Author's Note

The 25th of June 1975 is known as the darkest day in Indian politics.

On this day, then-President Fakhruddin Ali Ahmed, proclaiming the country to be in danger, passed a decree known simply as the 'Emergency'. The once golden India turned into a grey widow, slowly falling apart in the hands of a tyrannical government. Indira Gandhi, the Prime Minister at the time, had a case running against her at the Allahabad Court where she was accused of corruption and election fraud. Gandhi challenged this in the Supreme Court of India, where she received a conditional stay on the verdict. This gave her the power to postpone all state and parliamentary elections and remain in power. Television programs, radio broadcasts and newspapers were under regulations and examined thoroughly for anything written against the Gandhi government.

Many people, including politicians, were thrown in jail, depriving them of their basic democratic rights.

With Indira Gandhi in power, her son Sanjay Gandhi was free to exploit her position. He started a big campaign called 'Infertility', under the guise of family planning. Though it was maintained that people had the option to participate in the program, this choice was often taken away. Men were picked up from their homes in the middle of the night and taken to makeshift infertility camps. There they were forced to have an operation which resulted in complete sterilization.

In 1976 the biggest cleansing of Delhi slums to date occurred under the idea of 'Swachh Bharat', a phrase meaning 'Clean Delhi'. This act was intended to forever eradicate slums in Delhi. The cleansing was so brutal that police were ordered to shoot people on sight if they protested the 'Housing Demolition Order'.

The 70s were indeed dark times in Indian history, and not just because of the Emergency. The rising tension between Pakistan and Bangladesh ultimately led to a war. India helped Bangladesh to a victory on 26 March 1971, which resulted in millions of refugees crossing the border of Bangladesh into India. This created a huge budget deficit.

Then there were the droughts. It was as if even Mother Nature was turning against the government. The country was at its highest population inflation, the economy was in recession, there were strikes and high unemployment. The already vast divisions between the rich and the poor were widening. The country entered its worst phase – everything that could lead to growth would be stunted by lack of strong leadership. The image of a broken country with nothing but social divisions and poverty was just a facade – inside it the people were burning up for change.

The state of emergency in India lasted for two years, coming to an end on the 21 March 1977.

Water From Your Spring

What was in the water that candle's light
That opened and consumed me so quickly?

Come back, my friend! The form of our love
Is not a created form.

Nothing can help me but that beauty.
There was a dawn I remember.

when my soul heard something
From your soul. I drank water

from your spring and felt
The current take me.

by Rumi – *The Essential Rumi*
Being a Lover
From the six-volume poem titled Mathnawi

30 August 2017, 8:30 pm

I WAS RUNNING TODAY. I couldn't look back; it would only make me weak. Tears of shame rolled out of my eyes. I couldn't comprehend it; was it the cold winter wind or my own emotions that were the culprit?

People were staring; Tram 112 nearly hit me, dinging its bell as it drifted past, leaving a trail of traffic in the busy weekend rush. I regained my composure and waved my apologies to the tram driver.

The kohl in my eyes was smudged by the tears. I was exhausted. When ordinary people become victims, they become victims to their own situation – to their own sanity.

I wanted to be alone where no one could see my eyes. The light was slowly fading and the clouds that were swelling with rain would burst open any moment. I usually loved the rain.

All around me was the busy weekend rush. I could hear laughter, and outside a Vietnamese restaurant a man was playing his guitar. He played the same tune everyday but today I couldn't remember it.

As I was passing the restaurant I saw a familiar waiter standing outside, waving at me with a smile, thinking I might come in for dinner like every night. I looked away and lowered my head, taking the beanie out from my bag and resting it on my head like my crowning glory.

I started running to a lifeless street. I couldn't take the glory of happiness anymore. The street was deserted so I rested on the back of a car. I did not stop because the street was empty; I stopped because of the sharp pain that churned through my abdomen, slowly engulfing my entire body. I collapsed on the side of the car with my eyes shut and whispered a silent prayer.

My apartment wasn't far away; I could still make it to the other side of the road and catch Tram 96. I turned my body onto the left side, trying to bring some comfort to my pain. I held my breath for a few seconds and released it to see if the pain had made peace with me for a while. Thankfully it had.

I pushed myself off the ground, resting one hand on the car for support as I managed to balance myself off the ground. I walked rapidly, my left hand still clutching my abdomen. I walked fast before the pain could return.

***

It was very cold when I entered my flat. I made my way towards the bedroom, threw myself on the bed and stared at the empty ceiling. Reaching for the tallboy on the right hand side of my bed, I opened the middle drawer. My fingers were searching for the stack of smokes that I kept hidden for emergencies.

I lit a cigarette and ducked underneath the bed to get the ashtray out. I once again looked up at the empty ceiling; it appeared to be a projection of a film, showing my life and revealing the secret lives of real characters that unfolded with a letter.

Was it my misfortune that led me to what I am today, or had the part already been written for me to carry the burden of my modest past? Where did I come from? Where was this all leading to?

The hustle and bustle of city life made me fight for survival from day to day, but that left me hanging with a question: is there a present or a future for me?

The cigarette in my hand was fading into ashes and I quickly butted it out before any ash reached my newly spread quilt. I covered my face with my hands. I could still smell the stains of nicotine.

I was used to this feeling, but today it ran deeper. A new wound seemed to open up, mocking me. Where was my peace?

My thoughts were interrupted by a sudden thud from the lounge room. I sprang up from my bed and made myself head towards the lounge with the faint trepidation that someone could be in my flat. I switched on the light to find it was only a misplaced lamp beside the television, which had dropped to the carpet. I laughed at my surreal foolishness.

I opened a bottle of wine, drinking straight from the bottle as I returned to the bedroom looking for my bag. I took out the letter that Dorothy had given me earlier today when I went to visit her in the hospital. In her last days, suffering from cancer, she decided to torment me with the past; oblivious to my feelings, she found her peace.

I'd read the letter almost five times in the last twenty-four hours but I would read it again to make sense of it all. *Please forgive me, release me from this debt.* What about me? Who would release me from mine?

I looked at the photo she had enclosed with the letter. In the photo, I saw my nanny and a man. I'd seen him somewhere – but where?

I felt angry and remembered my nanny's words: 'Never do things that you regret in life.' Was it her way of covering her guilt? Or was I reading too much into her small fraction of humility? I was in such a predicament today – should I forgive and forget? Let bygones be bygones?

But, no – today the regrets ran deep, deep enough to seek revenge. Perhaps … vengeance, yes! Vengeance is the right word. The betrayal ran deep. I took a big gulp from the bottle.

The wine wouldn't work tonight – I needed more to ease the pain and rest my solitude. Then I looked at the photo – I'd seen it before.

I looked around the room and this time I smiled not on my foolishness, but at my wickedness. I picked up the sharpest knife from the kitchen, admiring how shiny it looked under the kitchen light. What would happen if blood oozed out from me and stained the carpet below? Would it be red or brown? What is the true colour of blood? My eyes, foggy and obscured with tears, fixed onto those two images in the photograph. I heard someone open the door, a voice calling out – I wanted to look back to see who was coming but I couldn't, my legs were heavy. Losing my balance, I fell to the ground and whispered, 'Vengeance, it shall be now.'

1975–1987

Life by the River Ganges

'ROSEMARY, CAN YOU come in here, child?' the matron ordered a frail, bruised, pale, young girl, who stood out among her dark-skinned fellow orphans as they were paraded every Sunday for a suitable sale.

Every Sunday the children would be bathed and dressed with clean fresh clothes that were usually washed the very next day. Sundays were always a big procession, a make-believe presentation so the buyers visiting the orphanage, wanting to make a diligent purchase, would have the privilege of a clean smell and not the ghastly stink of an orphan from the slums.

It was different today, as the buyers were different. The buyers were not the local families who came seeking a child; they were not there because they could not afford to pay for IVF in the West or because it was fashionable for the rich, as this was the 80s. The buyers today were foreigners.

***

The orphanage was famous around the city for Rosemary. She made headlines in the local news. It was a miracle when a blue-eyed baby with fair skin was found on the doorstep at this God-forsaken orphanage, which felt no moral ethic to save the needy.

The matron Anita needed money to run her family and the orphanage. The orphanage was left to her in an inheritance by her grandfather in the late 60s. The cracked walls and the holes in the roof already told the story of its ruin. Anita had to survive, so with the help of a midwife, she combed the city clinics which performed illegal abortions. These clinics would often sell her news of which rich family was trying to hide a pregnant daughter in the family – after a generous donation made to the pharmacist by Anita, of course. In return Anita would blackmail these families. It was the 70s; people would go to all sorts of extremes to protect their family name. Hence, after nine months, the labour of love was rightly owned by Anita.

The baby in return formed a good source of income for Anita and the orphanage named Karma.

Anita hired some greedy social workers who would supply her with buyers. People visiting the orphanage would always want to see Rosemary out of curiosity or inquisitiveness. The more people showed interest, the more Anita would raise the price. It was so expensive for the common family to buy Rosemary out that they would have to shift their interests to the common babies. The price was still too much – no room for bargaining. Thus, the profits would be shared equally between Anita and the social workers.

But Rosemary was not brought to Karma by Anita; she was left outside the door of the orphanage by someone unknown, wrapped in a white cotton sheet within a cot. A note was attached to a sprig of rosemary. It read: 'Her name is Rosemary.' Anita was confused by the statue of Mother Mary. Carefully picking up the infant in one hand and the glass milk bottle on the other, Anita was unable to justify to herself any appropriate name other than 'Rosemary' for the infant.

In return, when Rosemary turned five, Anita desperately needed money for survival. Rosemary's blue eyes, pale skin and angel smile planted an idea in Anita's mind.

'The English have left us with nothing after twenty-eight years of independence, a broken country and a poverty to live forever. Won't you be my Queen Victoria and rule the city for me?' Anita ran her fingers over Rosemary's hair, who was smiling at her comment. She had no idea what Anita's words meant. She was only five.

***

Aged twelve, Rosemary often wondered why she was different. The other children were dark and she was the fairest of them all with her striking blue eyes. She spoke the same language as the others and swore with the same enthusiasm. She was a rebel and would secretly smuggle cigarettes from the cook's son and sell them to the other girls and boys in the orphanage. The children would buy each cigarette for fifty paise from Rosemary, with the alms that they received from the city's rich who would come to the orphanage to make donations. Perhaps some were seeking redemption for their sinister souls. Rosemary would also make a marginal profit for herself, a mere two rupees after paying the cook's son. With the profit, she would buy some samosas from the roadside vendor outside the orphanage and share it with her close inmates.

This was a daily Sunday ritual for Rosemary, so she could escape the ghastly dhal and chapattis of the cook's menu. The menu was never improvised and always lacked the freshness of a home cooked meal. It was believed by some that the matron added sleeping pills to the dhal so that the 'inmates' of Karma would be disabled from making any sort of scrupulous plans for an escape. It was a trick used to put them off balance – to keep the already malnourished children drifting in and out of sleep throughout the day. Sunday was an activity day free from learning and cleaning. A free day meant for thinking about freedom.

Rosemary was clever and vigilant, always keeping her ears and eyes opened. Once when she was passing through the kitchen, she saw Anita adding a white substance to the huge pot of dhal that the cook was brewing on the clay oven. Her suspicions were confirmed. When lunch was served she signalled her friends not to touch it.

Ruma, belonging to the matron's camp, noticed this week after week: Rosemary, Neeru, Anil and Chennu not eating the dhal. Ruma decided to keep a close eye on Rosemary.

During one Sunday morning prayer outside the lawn, Rosemary made an exit. Anil and Chennu stood close to each other to conceal Rosemary's escape through the gate to the vendor. No one saw her – except for Ruma.

***

There was no one on the lawn when Rosemary came back. 'Rosemary!' She heard Anita's voice and tried to run. 'Shabana, chowkidar – catch her,' Anita ordered the ayah and the caretaker.

Shabana, the ayah, froze; she watched helplessly as the chowkidar grabbed Rosemary and took her to the matron's office.

Anita took out her whip and lashed in front of Rosemary. 'Where will you run from me, my Queen Victoria? Don't let another sin rock your life, otherwise I will have every right to destroy yours.'

Rosemary was still wrestling with the chowkidar, who was holding her tight. There was fear and anger in her eyes but she was determined to break free. 'You're a liar. I know what you mix in the dhal.'

'You cheap mongrel, how dare you speak to me like that.' Anita came closer to Rosemary. 'Shabana, strip her and throw her on this table ... she will know what happens when one disobeys the rules of Karma.'

'No, *Didi* (sister), please don't do this, I beg of you, please.' Shabana looked at Anita, her eyes pleading for mercy.

'Shabana, do what I am saying if you still want to be employed here.' Anita, disgruntled at Shabana's request, walked out of the room.

A nervous Shabana, with tears in her eyes, hesitated before slowly walking towards Rosemary. Shabana's hands trembled as she undid one button at a time on Rosemary's frock.

'It's okay, Shabana bi, it's not your fault.' Rosemary smiled at her.

Shabana was astounded with so much maturity from a twelve year old girl. She stripped Rosemary on the table and ran outside to escape the felony that Anita was about to commit.

Rosemary screamed at the first lash and the second, and she continued until she received ten lashes. When blood surfaced from the wounds, Anita stopped. 'Shabana, come here you wretched woman. Take her and get ready for the evening. Hide her whip marks, you understand? I am finally expecting some decent money from my Queen Victoria's sale.'

Shabana hurried back into the room, her eyes filled with tears; she picked up the half-dead body of Rosemary.

'Do whatever you have to do with her, just get her ready by five. Make sure you hide her scars and she's able to walk. Go past the kitchen and ask the cook to send in my lunch. I am hungry. Now get out.'

***

It was already three when Rosemary woke up; her moaning in pain woke Shabana. 'Here, my child, have some water.' Shabana took Rosemary on her lap and handed her a glass of water. She raised the frock to see the wounds from the whip; Shabana closed her eyes in disbelief. 'Let me get the Betnovate cream and apply on your back. It will burn at first, my darling, but you are brave, naah!'

'I am.' Rosemary nodded her head in approval.

While Shabana applied the antiseptic cream, the burning sensation left Rosemary whining in pain. Shabana closed her eyes. 'Come my dear, you sit up while I go and fetch you some milk before the cook wakes up. Then we will both make plans to dip Matron Anita into the Ganges to wash off all her sins.' They both laughed.

After eating, Shabana plaited Rosemary's hair and bowed the ends with red ribbons. She held her hand and took her to the line formed by the children of Karma Orphanage waiting to be chosen for a suitable home. Rosemary was unbelievably strong to withstand the pain.

***

'This is Rosemary, for whom we have become so famous around the world,' said Anita. 'I am so humbled that you have come so far from the land of Big Ben to be here, Mrs Smith.'

'Not from there – it doesn't matter where I come from,' Mrs Smith corrected Anita. 'So, when can we have the documents ready? I have the money.'

'What's the rush? Papers can be signed later; she is yours after we exchange the money.'

'Here, two hundred thousand rupees in cash. This covers the ayah too. I want her with the child,' Mrs Smith sternly replied to Anita.

Anita was openly confused by this sudden request. When Mrs Smith explained that she was looking for a nanny to care for the girl, Anita said, 'Absolutely, Shabana has brought Rosemary up since the girl was an infant. Perfect, it's all settled then, but you have to understand we will be at a loss without her. These days it's very difficult to get such good ayahs.'

'Two hundred and fifty thousand rupees – no more. I will come tomorrow to fetch them both. Have them ready by eleven.' Mrs Smith exchanged looks with Shabana and Anita. She dropped the cash at the table, then left.

***

'Memsahib, Anita Memsahib, come quickly, police is here,' the chowkidar screamed.

Anita quickly stashed the money from the previous day in the cupboard and locked it. 'What's the matter, officer?'

'We have found a body at the *chowk*, people on the road recognised her by dress as one of the ayahs working here. The body is still lying at the *chowk*, it will be tough to recognise as the face is totally disfigured, skull crushed under the lorry and the torso badly damaged.'

Anita hurriedly followed the policeman to the *chowk*, cursing away under her breath while stashing some money inside her blouse. On her way to the gate she told one of the ayahs to tell Shabana to get

Rosemary ready quickly. Mrs Smith would be here shortly.

'Yes, it's her! She worked for me.' Anita recognised the white sari with the blue border and after a closer look she recognised the cross around the body's neck. Anita was puzzled. She overheard the vendor giving a statement to the constable that Shabana was running across the busy street without noticing the lorry coming from the other side of the road. Anita quickly placed three hundred rupees into the policeman's hand. 'I don't want anything to do with this.' The policeman nodded in approval. Anita hurried towards the orphanage.

Mrs Smith arrived at 11.00 sharp, waiting for Anita at her office. Anita slowly wiped the sweat from her forehead as she smiled wryly at Mrs Smith. 'Unfortunately, there has been a small incident … the ayah, Shabana, met with an accident today. Umm … what do we do with the money?'

'Keep it. Give me Rosemary, I want to leave now.' Mrs Smith tried her best not to be shocked. However, Anita was now content.

They signed the documents, dated 31 August 1987. She handed over the documents to Anita and waited for Rosemary in the lobby.

Rosemary was dragged along by one of the ayahs of the orphanage. 'I want Shabana bi, I want Shabana bi, where is she?'

Anita hurried towards her and raised her eyes to Rosemary. 'Now be quiet, she has gone to fetch her belongings, she will join you later. Quiet now! Say your goodbyes to everyone and meet me in the lobby in ten minutes.'

***

Chennu and Anil, the two boys, looked sad but they were pleased as Rosemary was going with her own kind – while Neeru looked at her with contempt. The boys hugged Rosemary and exchanged a few tears. Neeru ran away when Rosemary came to hug her. She was crying too.

Rosemary looked at Neeru for a very long time until her figure vanished behind the eucalyptus tree in the courtyard.

16 March 1974

Ted

'DAMN, IT'S HOT HERE!' Twenty-four year old Ted Smith wiped the sweat from his forehead with his handkerchief while standing outside Dum Dum Airport, waiting for the car to take him to the foreign office.. The air around him was suffocating; for Ted it was a dreadful change from the cold weather of Melbourne. The heat seemed to have absorbed him totally, his shirt drenched with sweat. He was suffocating from his own body odour. He took out his hat and tried to cover his head and then his nose with the wet handkerchief, protecting himself from the polluted air.

God, what am I doing here? he thought.

***

Theodore Smith was born 16 January 1950 to a rich politician's family, well known to everyone in the elite circles of Melbourne. His grandfather, Richard, ran a sugar mill in Mossman, Queensland, which was a traditional business handed over from one generation to the next. When Theodore was born to John and Dorothy Smith, they decided to move to Melbourne for their only child's education.

Richard Smith was also heavily interested in making his career in politics, and would often ask his son John Smith to come to Queensland on a fortnightly basis to help his father out.

In 1957, the legacy of Queensland leader Vince Gair came to an end and, along with that, came the fall of the Queensland Labor government. Gair was brutally voted out. To cut his losses, he had to shake hands with the DLP. Ultimately, in 1962, the Queensland Labor Party was assimilated into DLP.

There was little hope for John Smith as his father Richard suffered, finding himself caught in the vicious cycle of business, political turmoil and family life. Richard's wife remained in seclusion because of this and her poor health. No doctor or nurse could look after her as she yearned to be with her husband, son and grandchildren. Richard's wife, John's mother, was dying of loneliness. No one seemed to understand that; on the contrary, John Smith wanted to run away from his father's politics for some family life. Things changed quickly for John and his family. John Smith had to leave for Queensland as his mother's health deteriorated and she grew seriously ill. His father needed him. From that day, for three years he travelled.

The day Ted Smith turned twelve in 1962, John Smith decided that he was old enough to be left in a boarding house. Dorothy and John moved back to Queensland to take control of the business.

Richard injected more money into the campaign for his own selfish motives. But it was all in vain: Gough Whitlam won the 1972 federal election. The quick thinking of DLP's plan of action kept the ALP out and pushed them to the periphery. Richard had to surrender and moved his campaign with the Whitlam government, as he lost his seat in the ALP. John Smith was relieved for a while that his father finally decided to slow down – but Richard left no stones unturned for John not to help him get started with his new political campaign. Without any warning John Smith found himself caught in the political dramas. John got used to the political attention he got from his peers, especially when his father supported him. Dorothy was also very happy at her husband's sudden change and enthusiasm on his political career.

But life is unpredictable sometimes. John and Dorothy Smith decided to sell the family business after John's father passed away; they brought his legacy down to Victoria. Dorothy kept Richard's dreams alive for John to pursue his career in politics. They also couldn't be happier, being close to their son in Melbourne. When Ted graduated from high school he was excited to learn about his family background, including his grandfather's legacy as a politician under the Labor Party in Queensland.

John Smith couldn't be happier to see his son's thirst for learning more about the family, as he wanted Ted to carry the Smith name further on in politics.

Ted completed university with a Bachelor of Arts, majoring in economics and political science. Both Dorothy and John supported his choice. John had revisited his father's political dreams, not by choice but by helplessness. John's future had already been written by his father and wife; it's not that he was never interested in the family business or politics, but he wanted to be close to his son. John had missed his father when he was growing up and was always left with a nanny. The only time John was happy was when his father would pick up the football and kick a goal with him – but sometimes that would be cut short, as soon as there was a trunk call from the political party or a crisis emerged at the oil rig. But, John Smith was glad that he was there for his son Ted; he was there when Ted took his first step to walk, when he fell down and broke his ankle, on his first day of school, on every summer and Christmas break. John Smith was always there for Theodore Smith.

What Richard couldn't do for John, John did for Ted. John not only did an outstanding job as a father but also played the ultimate politician as an emerging MP – with a little persuading by Dorothy. Dorothy tasted power and fame during Richard's campaign and she knew her husband was not a born businessman like her father-in law. She had to take control of things for her and Ted. She fought pillar to post gaining confidence from the Whitlam's government to pursue a campaign for John for Toorak. John Smith was ready to campaign for Labor in the upcoming election on 18 May 1974 for the Kew seat.

After Ted graduated from high school, he opted for a job as an intern in the Department of Foreign Affairs. Ted's father was influential, but it was not because of John that Ted scored a job at the ministry, instead demonstrating he was hardworking and had his own talent in politics. John Smith already recognised this and was very satisfied at his son's choice.

In November 1973 there was a post for a financial operations officer position available in the foreign office in Calcutta, India, to be filled by March 1974. There were few enquiries for the post as most people preferred Europe – at the time the political condition of India was unstable. In the beginning of 1973, the Indian Prime Minister Indira Gandhi's popularity began to decline. People's expectations were unfulfilled, especially those in rural areas. There was urban poverty and economic inequality, and the government did nothing to eradicate or lessen the social burden of caste and class oppression in the countryside. The country had already suffered one war recently with Pakistan to give independence to Bangladesh; drained foreign exchange reserves weren't far behind, creating a severe deficit. There were famines as monsoons failed for two consecutive years during 1972 and 1973, leaving most parts of the country, especially rural Bengal, with massive shortages of food and inflated local prices.

Ted knew about the conditions. His father helped him get the inside news. He understood that there could be repercussions in the UN if India failed as a country; there could be emergency situations where Australia might have sanctions imposed on India, and so Ted should be on call to fly back to Australia at a moment's notice. He thought of the pros and cons, but he saw this as an escape. Ted jumped at the proposition; although he was not inclined to the location either, the thought of serving at a foreign office would not only be great for his career, but also to escape from the family. Dorothy was not at all happy with this idea, but gave in when her husband declared it was great for his son to start his political career – it would toughen him up.

Ted's parents had no clue to his loneliness. He had no siblings, so it was him and only him who was expected to carry his parents' wishes forward. He wanted to be a teacher, always fascinated with the idea of literature, but when he asked about teaching at the age of twelve his mother already made a point to him: 'Oh Teddy, teachers make a poor salary! You are my son, you *will* be a politician. One day.'

Ted always struggled with his mother and father's ideas and it was hard for him to understand the purpose of his creation. He always thought he was created by his parents for *their* ultimate purpose, to fulfil *their* dreams.

'Take the vaccines and be careful of not eating anything from outside; the country is in dire straits, make sure you be careful,' Dorothy Smith said politely to her son at the breakfast table.

Ted obeyed with a nod.

'Son, send me a telegram when you speak to the chancellor in Delhi. And any problem with the accommodations, let me know,' John added.

Ted liked the idea of his parents being so overprotective but was also looking forward to a break from this, where he wouldn't be told how to do everything – especially minding his life. It was a change he was welcoming. Having no siblings made it impossible to breathe in that household sometimes. Though John would always be there for him, Ted wanted freedom. He often wondered when was the last time they smiled together as a family without being told what to do. His father's ideas were always forced onto him very swiftly, with the help of Dorothy.

Ted was an attractive looking man; his tall masculine body at the age of twenty-four was a credit to the swimming lessons that Dorothy forced onto him. His father also ran with him every morning. But despite all the wonders of being a healthy man, he lacked skill in social interactions. No matter how he tried to be resourceful in the company of women with his blue eyes and a charming smile, he knew sometimes it was hard to win a woman's affection with these attributes. He needed to make conversation.

Seeing his son's predicament, Dorothy tried to introduce him to some rich society women. But Ted found it equally hard to associate with them. These women were all interested in high tea, tennis, cocktail parties and which frock matched their diamonds or pearls. No one was interested in listening to a verse from Shakespeare; no one was interested in going on a rowing expedition with him on the Yarra or driving with him to Sorrento, or seeing the city of Melbourne under the moonlight. These society women thought that it was boring. Ted gave up on his search for the ideal woman – instead he searched for off-shore projects.

***

Squinting his eyes to the sun, he rubbed his brows. The sweat was making it difficult to see a man approaching him. 'Babu sahib, I am Jamshed, who will look after your stay at the house. I am the manager of all new interns.'

Ted looked at a short, fat, bald man. Ted was quite intrigued with his new companion, who spoke perfect English but with a strong accent. He was already accustomed to people carrying his luggage and today it was no different.

'It's so hot here, Jam …' Ted looked blankly at his new acquaintance.

Jamshed scratched his head and then smiled at him. 'Jamshed, like bread and jam and to park a car, the English calls it shed, so jam plus shed is Jamshed.'

Ted couldn't help but laugh at his sense of humour. *This guy is great. Simple but full of greatness,* Ted thought.

The traffic was chaotic, but the coolness of the air-conditioning in the white Ambassador car made it possible for Ted to connect with the outside world. A cycle-rickshaw came very close to their car; Ted turned to the rickshaw and behind him he saw a trail of cyclists with clay pots tied to them. *Is that safe?* He wanted to ask Jamshed what the clay pots were for, but then out of nowhere he saw a tram bulging with people stopping right in front of them, bringing traffic to a standstill. 'Tram? Is there a tram line here?' Ted looked at Jamshed curiously.

'Yes, sahib! These trams are, since 1902, run by the old Calcutta tramways company. There are twenty-five routes in total, goes from Shyam Bazaar … Sorry, how will you know? This is Shyam Bazaar.' Jamshed looked at his new boss apologetically.

The trams looked like little tin cans running on electric without any doors. Passengers could actually run alongside and catch the tram, or get off, without any inconvenience. He was surprised that this organised chaos, with millions of people and an electric tram line since 1902, constituted the largest tram system in Asia. The British empire created a marvellous plan just to create more chaos. Ted smiled at this thought.

He thought of the trams of Melbourne and how they had evolved over the years from being just like tin cans to softer seats and pneumatic doors. There were talks on making them fully air-conditioned in the coming years. Traffic jams blocked up Melbourne roads. The government hadn't lost their compunction with increasing their tram network, slowly pushing into the suburbs, but the public considered trams the poor man's choice, and instead nurtured their fascination with cars.

The thought of Melbourne made Ted nostalgic, yearning for home. He cleared his throat. 'How far is the office?'

'Sahib, we are now at Lal Dighi. This is the Writer's Building to your left, built by the British in 1777. It served as the office for writers of the British East India Company, hence the name. The West Bengal state government is thinking of making it as a secretariat.' Jamshed sounded like the perfect tour guide. Before Ted could interrupt he continued. 'Sahib, we will cross North Calcutta and take Chittaranjan Avenue and Jassore Road to beat the traffic – say another forty-two minutes. North Calcutta is just five kilometres from here. After your visit to the office I will take you to Lake Town, where you will be staying.'

Ted was relieved that he had Jamshed with him for all his Calcutta information.

The smell of polluted air and the stifling heat were enough to convince Ted to stay inside the air-conditioned comfort of the Ambassador. He shifted his gaze to the street around him and its total madness. People, trucks, buses, small cafes, vendors selling newspapers and roadside food where people were flocking to eat and buy cigarettes at the same time. What was extraordinary about all this were the tall buildings casting shadows across these streets.

In a corner across the street under the Writer's Building, there were men in white huddled up with banners in English and the native tongue: 'Desh Bachao (Save India) – We want her resignation.'

Ted was curious. 'Jamshed, what's that?'

'Oh! Sahib that's nothing – get used to these sorts of processions. That's Lok Nayak's people – he's a folk hero, one of the freedom fighters who fought the British. Now he says our Prime Minister is corrupt and wants her resignation.'

Ted nodded. 'Do I need to be worried?'

Jamshed smiled. 'No, babu sahib, you are a diplomat – you don't need to worry. Just be careful on the streets.'

Ted managed a wry smile. Taking his handkerchief out this time, he covered his nose from the urine stench coming from the wall across the street. No sign of a public toilet, so quite conveniently people used the wall for urinating. *That's the difference between living in Melbourne and in a third world country*, Ted thought.

By now Ted was not only tired but he was getting frustrated with everything, including Jamshed. 'How long to go to the house, Jamshed?'

'Just around the corner, sahib.' The car stopped outside a luxurious bungalow, with large pots of flowers outside the gate. Once outside the car, Ted looked up at the enormous house. The building had eight windows and each of them had the back of its air-conditioning unit facing outside.

'*Zor lagake haisha!*' someone shouted.

Ted turned to the commotion. He was horrified to see around ten men pulling a cart laden with boxes. 'Shite!' came from his mouth. 'Is that even safe?'

Jamshed laughed at his boss's whimsical face. 'Get used to these men, they are the movers and shakers of Calcutta. These labourers use this daily mantra to move offices, homes or even transport stuff to shops or godowns. This mantra keeps them going.'

'What do you mean?' Ted asked.

'What they are saying is give all your strength or apply all your force with whatever you have got. Zor meaning force, sahib.'

How extraordinary, Ted thought as they all sang in unison to work this daily grind under the punishing sun. 'What about trucks, Jamshed?'

Seeing concern in his employer's face, Jamshed put down the luggage and turned to his boss. 'Sahib, do you think that the potholes of the Calcutta roads can take such atrocities? It's a system that is coming from generations. Sahib, this is Calcutta – everything is easy here, you just have to leave everything upstairs.' He pointed his index fingers to the sky.

Ted looked up to see where Jamshed was pointing at – all he could see was the sky.

Jamshed tried to hold in a giggle but let it go, laughing at his boss's peculiar face and blowing a whistle. 'Sahib, up meaning Allah – God.' He didn't spare any theatrics and was as animated as he could be for Ted's entertainment.

Realising he was the joke, Ted quite appreciated his new companion. Raising both hands in the air, Ted walked towards Jamshed, which startled Jamshed, thinking that he might have upset Ted. On the contrary, Ted hugged Jamshed, whispering in his ears, 'Boy, am I glad to have you here!'

Jamshed was speechless – he didn't know if he was supposed to laugh or cry.

They approached the gate and a guard welcomed Ted as Jamshed screamed, 'Bhai gate kholo. Open the gate.'

Hearing his loud voice, two or more people came running from inside the huge elaborate house. They started organising the luggage with Jamshed.

'Sahib, this is Babu Ram, the caretaker of the bungalow … this is Lala jee, our cook … and this is Shyama Prasad, your laundryman. I am in charge of everyone here.' Jamshed mentioned this to Ted politely, as he didn't want to risk any of Ted's unusual behaviour.

It was almost another 500 yards to reach the main house; the outside façade was only plain offices. Once they reached the main courtyard, Ted learned the bungalow was rented by the Australian Consulate for another five years. The Australian flag was firmly placed inside the courtyard.

'Sahib, we are in the east wing, second floor of the bungalow.' Jamshed pointed to the porters who came rushing from inside. On taking the stairs, Jamshed continued his spiel, this time taking time so Ted completely understood. 'Sahib, the façade that you saw was the offices where visas are processed – primarily its only purpose is for accounts and bookkeeping. Your office and other babu sahibs don't sit here – that office is different where you will go tomorrow, where the actual visa enquiries are made. There is a discussion within the Indian government that these offices where the visas are processed will soon become one main office, so you don't all have to travel, and it's just one office. The living quarters are currently in the east wing and the west wing. When it happens the living quarters will be east wing and the offices west wing.'

Ted nodded in approval. 'Yes, I see.'

Jamshed quietly went in front of Ted to open the door of his room. 'This is your own private room, sahib. Lucky no one is here to share your room as most of them are on holidays.' Jamshed then ordered the porters to place his luggage near the main door.

'How many rooms are here in the east wing?' Ted asked, looking outside his window.

'Ten, sahib: one is with the embassy High Commissioner, which is right behind the east wing, and the other five rooms are for guests of other diplomats or their families. The other four rooms are for people like you to share who are single, sometimes the press, and so on.' Jamshed said that in one breath.

Ted nodded. 'What about the west wing?'

'West wing has five rooms for document-keeping purposes. Okay sahib, is there anything that you would like me to do? Dinner is at 7.30 pm.' Jamshed folded his hands.

'No, Jamshed, that will be quite alright. No dinner for me tonight, just have the air-con on for me and close the door behind you. If I need anything, I will ring you.' Ted extended his hand towards Jamshed for a handshake.

The handshake put Jamshed in an easy mood. He was so happy that his face flashed with a glowing smile.

17 March 1974

Jamshed

J AMSHED LOOKED at the huge clock hanging in the main corridor. It made a loud sound at the stroke of 7.00 am. *Should I wake him now?* Jamshed contemplated. 'Lala jee, how long for breakfast?' Jamshed screamed at the cook.

'Another 10 minutes, waiting for your wife to come to set the table,' Lala jee replied while frantically doing a double take on his French toast.

'Don't know if Mumtaz will come today, she was not feeling well last night,' Jamshed replied while tasting the French toast. He looked at the cook with a frown. 'Lala jee, please be careful with your extravagant hand in chilli. Mumtaz complained of bad gas the day before yesterday after eating your dhal.'

'What has chilli got to do with gas? Your wife must have eaten your beef curry. *Chee! Ram! Ram!*' Lala jee replied in his defence.

Jamshed's nostrils flared up in anger; he could feel his heartbeat rising and his forehead trickled with sweat. 'How dare you make fun of my wife?' Jamshed took a knife from the side of the kitchen.

Listening to this commotion, Babu Ram the caretaker came running to the kitchen. Seeing Jamshed and Lala jee ready to cut each other's throats, he screamed for help. 'Shyama Prasad jee, come quickly, the daily festivities have started in the name of God again.' Babu Ram ran towards Jamshed and Lala jee to save the knives before the kitchen was bathed in their blood. Shyama Prasad ran to Babu Ram's aid and they rolled in laughter, as they both knew it was an everyday routine.

Everyone knew about Jamshed's temper and how he once broke the leg of a thief trying to run away with his bag of groceries. It was nothing to do with groceries – in fact he had nearly lost a very expensive thing: a gold ring that he had been keeping for his then-only daughter Shabana.

***

Jamshed always dreamt of having a son and his wife Mumtaz couldn't deliver him one. He was disappointed with her and wanted to marry another woman from Bangladesh, but he could not leave behind everything in Calcutta to go to Bangladesh and live in a small village, exactly like the one from which he had run away from. Jamshed hated Mumtaz for it and blamed her for his unhappiness.

He was very close to being promoted from a simple handyman to become a head man at a construction site. As soon as Shabana was born he started to worry about getting her married. He had to have a lot of money for her wedding – and then when his wife gave birth to another stillborn girl, and later Razia was born, that was it. Jamshed enrolled himself into a night school and managed to educate himself.

In March 1944, Lieutenant General Ivan Mackay was appointed Australia's first high commissioner to India. The first consulate general of India was first opened as a trade office in Sydney in 1941 and soon after independence in 1947, small offices were opened in the main cites of India to serve as visa offices. In 1959, twelve years post-independence, many countries were beginning to build their foreign offices in India.

There was an advertisement in the newspaper – a caretaker wanted for a diplomat's office, English an important skill. Jamshed worked very hard. He came to know the habits, likes and dislikes of his foreign counterparts. Jamshed became a tour guide and also a peon of the foreigners living in the guest house.

When Australia's High Commissioner decided to rent the property for the consulate's office and living quarters for the diplomats, they decided to hire a manager. In October 1961, the High Commissioner advertised for a manager of the entire living quarters of the foreign diplomats. When word spread about this position, Jamshed left no stone unturned to get this job – he even invited his superior to lunch as a bribe. The superior not only wanted a lavish lunch but he made a further request for five hundred rupees to pay to the person who handled data for potential candidates. 'Just go to his office, Jamshed. He will open his drawer and quickly slide in an envelope. The rest I will take care of,' the supervisor whispered in Jamshed's ears.

Five hundred rupees was a lot for Jamshed; his monthly salary was only three hundred. But he wanted this job, not for him but for Shabana's future wedding. It was a respectable position and his salary would increase to one thousand rupees with a bonus every year; also, he would have paid accommodation in the servant's quarters at the back. The slum where Jamshed used to live was not ideal or safe for the growing girls. Mumtaz, Shabana and Razia all did *purdah*, covering their faces. He was concerned more for Shabana; she was growing up fast into a beautiful teenage girl. Mumtaz once complained to him that they needed him around the house, especially as the girls were growing up and the boys in the slums were getting very inquisitive about Shabana.

Jamshed had to arrange the bribe no matter what. He went to the jeweller and mortgaged his wife's jewels and silverware. Mumtaz couldn't protest about this as she had no say – she and her daughters depended on Jamshed.

It was not just the bribe that did the work but also Jamshed's efficiency. Jamshed enrolled both his daughters into English schools up to the tenth-grade metric. They all lived a modest life and Jamshed became engrossed with his work – he was now satisfied that his wife and his girls were safe.

When Shabana turned thirteen, Jamshed ordered Mumtaz and Shabana inside the living quarters of the High Commissioner to help the cook, as there was a need for additional help in the kitchen. Jamshed was responsible for all the hiring, so what better way to use the opportunity? He thought it was not only a marvellous idea to pocket some money, but it also kept his entire family near him. Every day after school, Shabana and Razia would come to the living quarters to help their mother and learn kitchen work, sometimes filling in for their mother if she was sick or out to visit any relatives.

After Shabana completed her matric exams, it was decided that she would not go back to school, and at the tender age of fifteen she started helping her mother around the house, taking care of her nine-year-old sister.

Years passed and Jamshed was happier than ever. Everything was working according to his plan: he had now collected enough money for Shabana's wedding and decided to find a suitable man for his daughter. *Who wouldn't marry her?* he thought. The school's English education was almost in name only; they stopped teaching everything in English after the eighth grade. But to Jamshed it was enough; as long as she knew her ABCs, then to Jamshed, Shabana was educated enough in English.

Shabana was not only a beautiful, homely girl, but also a domestic goddess like Mumtaz. Shabana became very popular among her cousins; not for all these attributes, but for her beauty. Jamshed wanted to marry her within the family and thought of his eldest brother-in-law's son, Salman. Jamshed heard that Salman was about to extend his tailoring business into export; as soon as the incoming contract money was dispersed, Salman would raise a two-storey pukka brick house in Park Circus. Being a popular suburb for the Muslims and Anglo-Indians, the alliance between Salman and Shabana was even more attractive to Jamshed. Moreover, Shabana would stay in her own grandmother's house. It was not *mahram*, which relieved Jamshed as he was a very religious person. Mahram forbid a blood relative to go into a sexual relationship, as it would be considered haram (forbidden).

'What do you think about Salman, Mumtaz?' Jamshed asked his wife hesitantly, thinking she wouldn't agree.

'What do you mean?' Mumtaz questioned back.

'I mean if we marry Shabana to Salman? She will be within the family. They are first cousins and your mother will be very happy too. She loves Shabana,' Jamshed said to Mumtaz, choosing his words carefully.

'But Jamshed, he is very old for Shabana. He is twenty-nine and Shabana is just nineteen,' Mumtaz replied sympathetically.

Jamshed looked at her angrily. 'So? Just ten years – you and I have sixteen years of difference. When I was thirty-one you were fifteen. That didn't matter to you, did it?'

Mumtaz now knew that Jamshed was getting very angry, but she was powerless in explaining to Jamshed that it was not okay with her when she was married to him. Mumtaz's father decided on the marriage because Jamshed was offering a one thousand rupee meher payment for her. The money was so attractive to Mumtaz's father that he didn't care about his daughter – she wasn't educated, and her father always believed that a daughter was only good for looking after the house. Once married she should take care of her husband and provide him with a son. Jamshed had repeatedly cursed Mumtaz and her father particularly as she had never been able to provide him with a son. After Razia was born, Jamshed took the meher back from Mumtaz's father.

Reflecting on this, Mumtaz held back her tears and looked at Jamshed with helpless eyes. She knew Jamshed could be cruel and cold. 'Very well then, if you think that's best for Shabana and if you have already decided, there's nothing much I can do.' Mumtaz knew that Salman was a good man, but he was old. She didn't want Shabana to go through the same struggle she had gone through – failing to produce a son.

***

'*Abba*, what are you doing? Keep that saucepan down!'

Jamshed turned his head to the voice. 'Shabana! What are you doing here?' Jamshed asked his daughter, lowering the saucepan carefully, slightly ashamed of what he was about to do.

'*Aami* (Mother) couldn't come to help Lala jee *chacha* (uncle) so she sent me,' Shabana replied to her agitated father.

Lala jee was pleased to see Shabana. 'Come here *beti* (child), help me set the table. Your father has gone mad, this is a daily routine for him.' Lala jee laughed now, his white face slowly returning to a healthy glow.

'Your mother still not feeling well?' Jamshed quizzed Shabana.

I will take her to the hakim in the evening and get him to give her some potion,' Shabana said.

'Take your mother to a good allopathy doctor and she will be okay, your father thinks your mother gets gas because of my extravagant chilli,' Lala jee cut in. '*Beti*, you are educated, tell your father it has nothing to do with my chilli and you believe in the hakim (Unani doctor).'

Shabana tried her best not to laugh; she knew Lala jee could say this because Jamshed was usually very polite in front of her. Shabana had to choose a hakim over a regular doctor because of Jamshed, but when he wasn't around she would go with the embassy doctor.

'By the way *beti*, congratulations on your engagement with your cousin. Where are the *mithais* (sweets)?' Lala jee continued.

'Careful Lala jee, Salman is no longer her cousin, he is her fiancé now. Be careful what you say next time! And sweets I will get with Mumtaz tomorrow.' Jamshed took over the conversation from Lala jee, pointing a spoon at him.

Lala jee, sensing that Jamshed was getting quite annoyed again, quickly changed the subject. 'Shabana *beti*, come and taste this French toast. Is the salt and chilli okay?' Lala jee looked at Shabana with helpless eyes.

Shabana gave a crooked smile and jumped at the proposal. '*Mast, chacha* (amazing, uncle) – it's very tasty, not at all spicy,' Shabana said teasingly, scorning her father with that comment. This was the only place where Shabana felt secure and unafraid of Jamshed, as she knew she had her allies: Lala jee, Shyama Prasad and Babu Ram.

Jamshed snorted at her comment. He looked at the watch and it was half past seven. 'I am going to wake up babu sahib.' He muttered something else under his breath in Bengali and left the kitchen. Halfway to the corridor he yelled out, 'Shabana, set the table and make sure you have your scarf on your head when you come to the dining area. Don't forget.'

Shabana was horrified that he had to yell this. She chose not to respond and just made sure she had her scarf on her head.

***

'Who is it?' Ted yelled at the knock on the door.

'Sahib, Jamshed. It's 7.30, breakfast is ready.' Jamshed waited for a reply and then he heard footsteps approaching the door. He saw a sleepy Ted, with some kind of mask on his head, opening the door to greet him.

'Good morning, Jamshed my man, how are you?'

'Good morning sahib, I am good. Breakfast is ready, would you like to join the others in the dining hall?'

Ted looked a bit surprised. 'Who else is there? You said no one else would be there.'

'Did I, sahib? There are still some people from the Australian consulate in Delhi and other people posted here. I said the High Commissioner is not here.'

Ted removed his eye mask. He seemed a bit annoyed with himself; rushing to his room, he ordered Jamshed to close the door behind him. 'Give me ten minutes, I will meet you at the breakfast table.'

Jamshed did as he was told and with a slight laugh at his new boss he muttered to himself, '*Sala pagla firang* (mad white man)!'

The dining table was laden with food, all from Australia – from butter to jam to Milo to Vegemite. They joined teabags, eggs, cornflakes, fruits, juices, biscuits and Lala jee's French toast: bread battered with egg and spices and served with tomato sauce. Jugs with milk and condensed milk occupied the side of the huge mahogany table.

'Good morning sahib,' Jamshed and the whole kitchen sang in unison.

'Good morning,' Ted replied. Screening the room, he sensed either he was too early or way too late. 'Where's everybody?' Ted looked at Jamshed, then Lala jee.

Before Jamshed could say anything, Lala jee quickly jumped into the conversation. 'Sahib, you were the last one, they hardly ate anything. Come, sit – let me serve you my French toast.'

Annoyed with Lala jee's quick remark and slightly ashamed by his manners, Jamshed leaned forward to serve an empty plate to Ted.

Ted was slightly confused with the whole scenario. He sat alone at the huge twenty-seater dining table, taking the plate from Jamshed. Slip, slop and flop! The French toast fell on Ted's plate. The insult carried on further by slathering his plate with tomato sauce. Jamshed was horrified and he closed his eyes.

On the contrary, Ted thought that it would be quite rude not to accept his hospitality. He waited until Lala jee finished what he was doing, then he took his knife and fork to cut through the egg toast. With precision, he cut the toast in four pieces, carefully dipping each piece in the sauce.

This is it, Jamshed thought. *At any moment, Ted sahib will run away to the toilet or will be gulping jugs of water.* He walked towards Lala jee, silently hissing at him and rolling his eyes. From the corner of his eyes, Jamshed could see Ted's face turning red – but he was eating.

'It's quite delicious, what is it? And there seems to be a little bit of spice,' Ted asked Lala jee.

Jamshed couldn't believe his ears. Lala jee winked at Jamshed and stuck his tongue out. That infuriated Jamshed.

'It's so ghastly in its appearance but amazingly delicious. Why is this called French toast?'

Lala jee quickly jumped to explain this. 'Sahib, I was working with a very famous Indian chef, he went to a foreign country called French.'

'You mean France,' Ted quickly corrected Lala jee.

Not knowing the difference, he continued with his culinary expertise. 'Yes sahib – French, France, same thing. What you do, sahib, you beat two eggs, throw in some of your country's cheese, salt, pepper, chilli and dip the bread into the eggs and fry it away. If you prefer some other spices then you can add that too. Hopefully some onions can do some wonders.'

Ted looked at Lala jee with his mouth open. He was tempted to try but scared about the spices; he'd heard some horrid stories back home about chillies and gastronomical disasters. Clearing his voice, Ted had another fork of Lala jee's toast and asked him, 'What spices are actually in here?'

'I just added some red chilli powder, cumin powder and loads of ga—'

Jamshed interrupted Lala jee with a frown. 'Lala jee, sahib will like it, don't worry – you just go and look after the kitchen, Shabana may need your help.' Jamshed was firm and looked at Lala jee with rage.

Quietly adjusting his posture, Lala jee took his body off the wall and made his way to the kitchen. Ted, wondering at the animosity between the two, didn't understand the rivalry between religions just yet. Just as Ted was about to take a forkful of French toast he heard Lala jee scream back, 'Sahib, it's garlic there and fresh coriander.'

'Lala jee, will you just get on with your work in the kitchen? Sorry you had to hear all of this, sahib. I am extremely sorry. I will have a word with him.'

'Oh Jamshed, relax mate, he's harmless.'

Jamshed scratched his head, confused by Ted's statement; he just nodded and immediately took his leave to head towards the kitchen for the rest of the afternoon meal.

***

Still angry with Lala jee for the morning's episode at the breakfast table, Jamshed was quietly brewing with anger and suffocating himself with a plan to humiliate Lala jee. Everybody was quiet in the kitchen as soon as Jamshed walked in. 'Shabana, go and clear the table and take this tea to sahib in his room. See if he needs anything. Don't forget to cover your head.'

'Yes *Abba*, I will do that,' Shabana replied quickly, covering her head with her *dupatta* (scarf) as she took a pot of tea to the sahib's room.

***

'Who is it?' Ted replied to the knock on his door.

'Sir, your tea,' Shabana replied.

'Yes, coming.' Ted opened his door to find a young woman with her eyes closed and her hands shaking with a tray full of pots. 'What's the matter?' he asked the woman, grabbing her trembling hands.

Terrified, Shabana let go of the tray with pots that came crashing on the floor. 'Ahaaaa!' screamed Shabana.

'What the hell is the matter with you, woman? Are you deaf or dumb?' Ted now clenched his teeth in anger.

Shabana quickly turned her back towards Ted and said loudly, 'Sir, you are naked, you're not wearing any underpants.'

'Blimey.' Ted looked down before saying nervously, 'Girl, haven't you seen a naked man before?'

Shabana ran downstairs, straight into the kitchen. '*Abba*, Lala jee *chacha*!' She tried to gasp for air to continue.

'What was that noise? Why are you running like that and where is the tray? What happened?' Jamshed asked.

'*Abba*, the tray fell from my hand, as I slipped. I guess sahib opened the door at the wrong time.'

'Shabana, you need to be careful with the crockeries, some of them aren't from the local Gariyahaat market. They are from Australia – if I have to give an inventory on stocktake, I don't want the white people to think we steal them.' Jamshed was angry now. 'Go upstairs and clean the mess – before that, make sure you take fresh pot of tea to him.' Jamshed's tone was very firm.

Shabana rushed with a broom upstairs. Carefully screening the lobby of the first floor, she looked for any naked man strolling in front of her. 'Thank you Allah!' Shabana spoke to herself when she saw Ted's room was locked. With her back towards Ted's door, she forgot that he could open the door to come out. Hearing the door squeak behind her, she felt her heart racing. *Let's not react,* she thought. However, it was too late. Shabana saw a shadow – *I dare not turn!* She could feel someone now sitting very close to her.

'Hi, I am extremely sorry for my behaviour,' a softly spoken Ted apologised.

Shabana, still having her back to Ted, replied, 'It's okay – just please don't tell the caretaker I saw you naked and that's why I dropped the pots.'

Ted stood there speechless for quite some time; he did not expect her to speak such good English. 'Where did you learn such good English? What is your name? You can look at me, I am wearing clothes.' Ted asked all these questions without taking a break as he was so excited to have an Indian cleaner speak to him in English.

Shabana slowly turned, carefully covering her head; she stood up carrying the remains of the broken pots. She kept her gaze down and slowly looked up at Ted. 'Sir, I learned English with the children here – Jim sahib taught me.' Shabana stopped to see the blank expression on Ted's face. 'My name is Shabana and I am Jamshed's daughter.'

'Hi Shabna … I am Theodore,' he replied with his eyes fixed on Shabana.

Shabana giggled and said, 'Sir, it's Shabana, don't worry, I will teach you.'

Ted laughed at her cheekiness. 'You can call me Ted too.' He winked.

Shabana laughed and began to run when Ted grabbed her hand. Shabana turned to break free from him but instead caught herself looking at Ted, who had his eyes fixed on her. Slightly embarrassed and shy at the same time, she gave a light push to Ted which made him let go of her hand. Shabana ran downstairs with her broom and the broken pots, laughing.

Ted continued to stare at her. His gaze followed her shadow until it disappeared behind the light. *What a lass,* he thought. The striking personality, the touch of her soft hand, her cheeky playful side and those mesmerising brown eyes that stood out against her slightly lighter skin. Ted couldn't believe it was Jamshed's daughter and that someone like her would intrigue him so much. Ted went back to his room realising that he completely made a fool of himself in front of her.

Ted was just settling himself in his room when he heard another knock at his door. Excited, he rushed to open the door only to see Lala jee's face. 'Sahib, your tea.' Lala jee handed Ted the pot of tray with a smile.

'Where is Shabna?'

Lala jee looked at Ted blankly. 'We don't … oh! You mean Shabana, Jamshed's daughter?'

'Yes, her, where is she?' Ted asked.

'Sahib, she's gone for the morning – they live here, we all live here at the back of the annexe at the quarters. Do you want something?'

Ted, realising that he was about to do or say something embarrassing, had to stop. 'No, nothing in particular – just surprised at her grasp of English. Was thinking it was good to converse with someone who can communicate back,' he said, taking the teapot from Lala jee.

'Sahib, I can communicate with you too. I even talk English.'

Ted chuckled. 'Of course, Lala jee, what would we do without you?'

***

Abba was right, he is a mad white man, Shabana thought that night. She was intrigued by his blue eyes. 'Razia, I met the mad white man today,' Shabana whispered in her sister's ear. She narrated the meeting. 'He stood there naked. I never saw a man like that – naked in one moment and the next moment he is grabbing my hand.' Shabana giggled.

'*Appa (sister)*, how is it to be touched by a man?' Razia asked.

'It was electrifying, but more than that, he has blue eyes. He looked like a doll you see in the market. Pale white skin and blue eyes. He looked just like that and when he winked, I know we have something in common … You kn—'

Razia stopped her. '*Appa*, the only thing that you have in common was both being cheeky. Don't forget you have a fiancé,' Razia said, rolling her eyes.

'Thanks Razia,' Shabana replied with annoyance. 'Of course I know that, but I am just having some fun. I never liked any guy but this white man is different.'

'Don't tell *Abba, Appa* – otherwise he will bury you alive,' Razia replied with a cautious tone.

Shabana laughed at her sister. 'Do you think I am not worried? I will be very careful.'

'So, you will continue to meet him?' Razia asked.

Shabana clapped her hands. 'Of course I will!'

'You are mad, Shabana Ali.' Razia laughed with her.

Soon they were interrupted by their mother's loud voice from the kitchen. 'Shabana, Razia, if both of you are done with your gossips and laughter, come and remember Allah too – pray to him to give you both some brains,' Mumtaz screamed.

15 March 1974

SHABANA DIVIDED HER HAIR into three sections: left, middle and right. She stood in front of the mirror, tying off her hair in a plait. She took a large chunk of black kohl, carefully taking the powder from the beautiful silver bottle that she inherited from her mother, which had been given to her by her grandmother. Now it was hers to inherit, as she soon would be Salman's fiancée.

She was hesitant for a while to dress up for her would-be fiancé, whom she'd called *bhai* (brother) all her life, yet in a few months she would be his wife, calling him husband. Like Mumtaz, she too was hesitant of this engagement.

She was educated till the tenth grade and spoke English, which was a big thing in the family and extended family as no one else spoke English other than Jamshed. Her English was good, because when she was in the sixth grade a missionary came to the Australian consulate for five years as a tutor, to teach the children living in the diplomat's office. Shabana would often hide behind the door in the corridor as her mother went to the kitchen to help Lala jee in the kitchen. The kids were so happy with the teacher, they were joking and painting, studying in groups and addressing their teacher not as 'sir' but by his name. *That is an interesting education,* she thought.

One day, Jim the teacher saw Shabana hiding behind the door. Being caught, she didn't know what to do – instead she ran away scared, fearing he would complain to Jamshed. As it happened, Jim called for Mumtaz and Jamshed to his office. 'Shabana, you rascal, come here,' Jamshed screamed when he got home afterwards.

Shabana dropped the hot iron that she was using to press her school uniform and came running, seeing both her parents in an angry mood.

'Who told you to go to Jim sahib's class?' Mumtaz added fuel to the fury of Jamshed's temper. Shabana could feel her cheeks burning and she was terrified of what would come next. 'From tomorrow you have been asked to attend classes with the white children after school.' Mumtaz looked at her angrily.

'There goes the extra income from the kitchen-hand,' Jamshed added in annoyance with his temper rising.

'Who told you to go there? You know we don't mix with them. Me and your father have agreed on one condition: every evening, after your classes with Jim sahib, you will help me with housework. On Saturday and Sunday, you'll work with Lala jee.' Mumtaz's voice softened.

Hearing this, Shabana ran to Mumtaz's arms.

Jamshed couldn't care less. He just went on cursing both of them. 'Say thank you to your mother, because of her promise for you to work with Lala jee on the weekends. I have agreed.'

Shabana couldn't thank her mother enough. For the next four years, Jim the missionary taught Shabana English after school. After her matriculation exams, Shabana could easily have gotten a job as a clerk, but her father would never allow it.

Shabana's eyes were cloudy with tears at the thought of her time with Jim learning English; she could see her kohl smudging. Quickly she took her *dupatta*, her long scarf, to wipe the sides of her eyes.

'Shabana, where are you?'

Hearing Mumtaz's voice, she quickly wrapped her head with her scarf and smiled at herself, looking at the mirror. 'Coming!' She ran to give chai to her fiancé and her grandmother with the extended relatives.

The family waited in Jamshed and Mumtaz's tiny one bedroom apartment, which was decorated with tiny fairy lights and flowers all over the balcony and the living room. '*Mubarak Ho*! Congratulations Jamshed and Mumtaz, from today my grandchild is now my daughter-in-law,' Mumtaz's mother screamed with enjoyment.

Shabana and Salman exchanged their engagement rings and Mumtaz's father forced Salman to take some jalebis. Salman's father and mother couldn't be happier to have Shabana as their daughter-in-law. Salman forced Shabana's mouth full with jalebi, stuffing it all the way through until she couldn't help but choke on them. She coughed hard and looked at Salman with disgust, her eyes watery with the cough – but in reality, that turned out to be a good excuse for her tears to roll out. They were tears about her life being over at nineteen, and the first thought of Salman choking her with the jalebis was enough for her to believe that she would be imprisoned for life. Shabana covered her mouth with her *dupatta* and ran to the kitchen where she wept in silence.

At night when the festivities were over, Shabana lay on the mat next to Razia, thinking over the whole evening. She hated Salman; he would be just like her father. They never had any interactions growing up, just the normal hello. She heard from her mother once that he used to hit Mumtaz with a stick and hated women who answered back to their men. She knew that she was leaving one monster's nest to be with another demon, in a marriage of compromise that sacrificed her dreams. She closed her eyes to think about her school life – how she missed it.

***

Shabana never complained, always keeping a smile on her face. Her beauty was in her simplicity and her innocence – both reflected on her physically. Shabana didn't know herself how beautiful she was, even as she received love letters from the boys in her class. She would throw them in the bin – not that she was uninterested, but because if her father found out, he would bury her alive.

She was a shy girl in school, but as years passed she began to revolt, especially against all the schoolboys. To her fellow girlfriends in school she would feel inferior of her status, but with Jim's education she felt far superior; when required, she was not hesitant to open her mouth to defend herself. Some of her classmates were quite scared of her direct personality. During lunch periods, she would sit in the shade at the back of the playground and eat her tiffin alone.

Once, one of her classmates wanted to teach her a lesson as she did not acknowledge his letter of friendship. During a sports class one day he decided to cover her chair with red ink. Soon after lunch it was the math test – all the children ran for their seats. When the test was over, everyone had to leave their copies on the teacher's desk. When Shabana got up the boy who inked her seat was the first one to whisper to the other boys, 'Look! Look! It's that time of the month, someone forgot her cloth piece.' The other boys turned to see her and were laughing hysterically.

That's odd, Shabana thought.

'There's blood on your uniform,' a girl sitting behind her whispered.

Shabana looked back in horror; she knew very well it was not blood. Touching her uniform, she felt her fingers wet and brought it up to her nose. 'It's ink,' Shabana screamed.

'Quiet class! What's going on?' The teacher screamed at the class. Shabana ran to the teacher and showed the boy's prank on her school uniform. 'Come here you two and give me your hands.' Taking the ruler out of her desk, the teacher marked both their hands with the wooden ruler.

When school finished Shabana knew the boy's father came to pick him up every day after school – she couldn't see let this chance go by. 'Oh! Uncle jee, I think your son left this letter for you.' She passed him the letter she had received from the boy. Confused, the man scratched his head.

The boy's father became furious; not because of what Shabana had given him, but because of his son's foolish letter to her. Shabana couldn't be happier than when she saw, from the corner of her eye, the father dragging the boy from inside the school and twisting his ears. 'That's why I am sending you to school, to be a romantic fool? The father drives a taxi and the son spends his money on romance.' It didn't hit the boy that Shabana was the one who had given his father his love letter.

The boy was not seen at school for the next few days. When he did return, he left Shabana alone for the rest of their days in school. The thought of that day made Shabana laugh.

She wanted to be an academic; once she asked Mumtaz if Jamshed would allow her to study further. 'You are not serious, Shabana? Are you? If I speak to your father for your further studies, he will stop what you are studying now as well.' Mumtaz reassured Shabana that for her, home duties was the best education.

'I hate them all,' Shabana cursed under her breath one night.

'*Appa*, go to sleep,' Razia said in a soft voice. 'You have work tomorrow with Lala jee, a new guest has arrived from Australia, *Abba* was saying he is very funny. *Aami* will not go, *Abba* doesn't know yet about *Aami* not going to work tomorrow. And you will have to do all her work too, so please sleep and let me sleep too.'

Shabana wiped her tears and looked at Razia. Caressing her head, she whispered, 'I will go to sleep, my little sister. I hope at least your dreams come true.'

'*Aamin*!' Razia said, giggling. Both sisters hugged each other to sleep.

***

A young girl in her late twenties, her hair pulled back in a tight ponytail with thick glasses, sat next to Ted in the dining table and was very inquisitive about Ted's father. 'Is your father John Smith, who is running a campaign for the local MP in Kew?'

Ted felt annoyed by the question as he was enjoying the chicken roast and potato salad during lunch – without Lala jee's ghastly French toast. 'Yes, he is,' Ted replied hesitantly.

'Oh, that is so exciting! We have a politician's son in the room, ladies and gentlemen.' The young girl spoke as if it was a public announcement to the fifteen people sitting in the dining area. Ted felt quite embarrassed with this, as if the entire room was buzzing with bees.

'Well! That's what we need now – a son of a politician.' There was a pin drop silence across the table. Ted looked in the direction of a very tall man with red hair and a light beard that covered some of his freckles. The man had his eyes down and smiled while cutting into his chicken. At first glance Ted knew he was off Ted's Christmas list. Ted's eyes fixed on him like glue.

'Oh Ted, this is James from Canberra.' The young girl in the ponytail continued to introduce Ted to everyone. 'Lastly, I am Cathy,' she said.

'Yes mate, you better have an alliance with Cathy, as I will be of no use to you.' James looked at Ted for the first time with a rude smile.

By now Ted was getting quite frustrated with this guy. 'If no one minds and takes it personally, I will just eat my lunch somewhere in peace.'

'Don't bother politician, I am done.' Pushing his plate towards Ted, James walked towards the door. Everyone looked at James in surprise.

'What's his problem?' Ted asked Cathy.

'He has a reputation for being quite explicit,' Cathy laughed.

Ted made a face. 'That guy doesn't even know me,' he replied, pushing his plate away – he'd lost his appetite for the roast. 'See you at the office tomorrow, Cathy.'

Just as he was about to walk out of the dining room, he saw Shabana standing in the corner with a towel next to the wash basin. Shabana winked at him. Ted was totally unaware that she saw everything that had just happened between Ted and James. Ted was pleased to see her and he pretended to walk towards the basin to wash his hands. Shabana, her gaze fixed on the other diners in the room, broke into a smile. 'What are you smiling at?' Ted asked, washing his hands with the soap next to the basin. His head was down, tilting his gaze towards Shabana.

'At you – if you wash your hands any more you won't need to scrub any other part of your body,' Shabana said lightly.

Slightly embarrassed, Ted shifted his gaze straight to Shabana; taking the towel from her hand, they stood looking at each other. Ted took the initiative to speak. 'Do you want to meet me later this afternoon in my room?'

Shabana was still looking at him as if she was in some kind of spell; without realising, she replied, 'Yes! Yes! I will be there.'

Ted winked at her, shoving the towel in her hand – as if waking Shabana from his spell, he made his way out snapping his fingers. Shabana smiled at his clicking fingers.

***

'Who is it?' Ted replied to the knock on his door.

'Shabana,' she whispered as low as possible.

Ted could barely hear. He looked at his watch. *Is it Shabana? It's ten past four*, Ted thought. He opened the door to a beautiful smile, glowing eyes, and a tray full of snacks and tea. 'What's this?' Ted asked Shabana.

'How do you expect me to come from the kitchen avoiding the suspicious eyes of my father?' Shabana replied, slightly annoyed. Ted stood there smiling with his hands crossed. Frowning, Shabana raised her head forward, pushing the tray towards Ted. 'Could you please now let me enter?' Shabana said, fretting.

Looking at her anxiousness and fear of Jamshed, Ted backed away to allow Shabana to enter. 'My apologies. Of course.'

Shabana looked to her left then to her right. Slowly taking two steps forward, she pushed the tray towards Ted again, signalling him with her eyes to take it inside his room. 'Oh! Okay,' Ted replied, taking the tray from her hands.

Shabana did one more check; kneeling down, she pushed her head in between the railing of the staircase and looked down to see if anyone was coming upstairs from the kitchen. She sat there on her bended knees in that awkward position, pushing her ears down to hear footsteps. 'One, two, three, four …'

Shabana's counting was interrupted by Jamshed's voice. 'Lala jee! Close the door behind me, I am going outside.' A sense of calm returned on Shabana's face when she heard Jamshed slam the door behind him.

She turned to look at a puzzled Ted. 'What's going on …?'

'Shhhh.' Shabana signalled Ted to go inside his room.

'Why?' Ted questioned.

Shabana pushed him into his room, locking the door behind her. She took her deep breath before closing her eyes and bursting into laughter. Seeing her hysterics, Ted pulled back from Shabana. 'What, are you scared of me now? Didn't you feel the adrenalin rush?' Shabana asked a nervous Ted with a smile. Their eyes met once again and this time Ted looked away from her. 'Yes! I knew it, you are scared of me. Why?'

Walking away from her, he looked outside his window – lost in the commotion of the moving world outside. Ted finally spoke. 'Yes! I am scared of you because I am not an expert in friendship with a woman. Especially with a commoner like you.'

'Oh! Really, that's an insult!' Shabana looked at him blankly.

'No! What I meant is that I've never had a relationship with a woman and you are different,' Ted tried to correct himself.

Shabana smiled. She walked towards him and placed herself between him and the window, blocking Ted's view of the outside. Taking Ted's hands in hers she said, '*The friend comes into my body looking for the centre, unable to find it, draws a blade, strikes anywhere. There is a light seed grain inside. You fill it with yourself, or it dies.*' Shabana paused, running her fingers on his hair she continued. 'I'm caught in this curling energy! Your hair! Whoever's calm and sensible is insane!' Shabana smiled as she looked at Ted, who was mesmerised with all this.

'That's beautiful – I have never heard someone speak so beautifully. Did you write it?' Ted asked.

'Rumi – it's written by Rumi,' Shabana said. 'He's a mystic Sufi poet from Afghanistan. The poem sounds even better in Urdu,' Shabana said.

Ted grabbed her closer to his face. 'This is perfect – will you teach me his verses? In Urdu? Bengali? Hindi?' Ted asked her.

'I will teach you Bengali, it will be handy.' Shabana laughed. 'Whatever pleases.'

Bringing Shabana close and cupping her face with both of his hands, Ted placed a kiss on her forehead. Shabana broke herself free from Ted's hands and shyly covered her face with her own hands.

Ted walked behind her and slowly whispered into her ear, 'Teach me Bengali and I will bring you books on anything you want to read.'

'Really?' Shabana turned her face to Ted in excitement. 'I wanted to study more but my father decided for me to work. I wanted to be independent ...' Shabana paused. Looking out the window she saw a kite caught up in a tree branch, trying to free itself. Pointing out the kite to Ted she continued. 'Look! That's me. At least the kite will fly away to its destination – the wind will help it. I have no one.'

'You have yourself to make that decision. Not your father,' Ted protested.

Shabana smiled. 'This is Calcutta. We are not rich like you, Ted sahib,' Shabana teased.

'Don't call me that, Shabana. It gives me an odd superiority complex that I am not used to. I tried telling your father too,' Ted said with a slight annoyance in his voice.

'Well! A while ago you called me a commoner,' Shabana teased.

Slightly embarrassed, he took Shabana's hands once again and whispered, 'Be not afraid of greatness. Some are born great, some achieve greatness, and others have greatness thrust upon them. I already apologised for that.'

'That's beautiful Ted, I want to read it. Do you have the book?' Shabana asked.

'It's from *Twelfth Night* by Shakespeare. He also wrote *Romeo and Juliet*, a beautiful love story. I will get it from the library for you,' Ted replied.

'Love story? What is the story about?' Shabana asked.

'You're serious – haven't you heard about *Romeo and Juliet*? It's about two young lovers and their tragic deaths, which ultimately reunites two feuding families.'

'Oh! It's like our Layla and Majnun. I see. They die a tragic death, reuniting two feuding families,' Shabana said excitedly.

'Yes, Shakespeare himself was inspired to write *Romeo and Juliet* from an Italian story. I'm not surprised that it has inspired Indian writers ...'

Shabana interrupted. 'No Ted, it wasn't written by any Indian – it's a 7th century Arabic story. I have a copy in Urdu.'

Ted was mesmerised by Shabana's knowledge about Urdu – pulling the chair next to the bed, he sat himself down. 'Teach me Bangla and Urdu, everything.'

Shabana laughed. 'No! No Bangla,' Shabana protested. Picking up the tray with the pots, Shabana signalled Ted to open the door for her. 'I'd better go now, otherwise people might get suspicious.'

'Why? You are my friend,' Ted protested.

'It's India, Ted. Bengali Hindu girls can have male friends by attaching a relationship to every man they meet, calling them "brother" on first name basis – whereas I am a Muslim girl and I am not allowed to have male friends,' Shabana said with a smile.

'Should we continue our lessons tomorrow – same time?' Ted questioned.

'Yes! I will come same time tomorrow,' Shabana replied, walking towards the door.

As she left Ted's room and turned to walk downstairs, Shabana came face to face with Cathy blocking her way. Cathy gave Shabana a look of disgust. 'What on earth are you doing in Ted's room, Shabana?'

Shabana's face went pale. Slowly recovering from the shock she replied, 'Oh! He wanted some tea.'

Cathy, still not convinced by the reply, signalled her fingers towards her eyes and then back at Shabana's. 'I am watching you, sweetheart.'

Shabana did not respond; she ran downstairs, scared from hearing Cathy break into a laugh.

'What's going on Cathy?' Ted came out of his room in response to the commotion.

'Oh, nothing Ted – just having some fun with that servant girl. These girls in India are so easily scared with a laugh,' Cathy said, looking at Ted and laughing.

Ted was not impressed with Cathy's attitude at all. 'Come on, Cathy, cut her some slack. Leave her alone.'

Cathy was horrified, yet she made no effort to say anything in her defence – she just looked at Ted and smiled. Ted was about to go to his room when Cathy said, 'It was just a joke. Relax!'

Better not to reply, Ted thought – closing the door, he just waved at Cathy.

Disappointed with Ted, Cathy walked away from Ted's room. 'You wretched girl,' cursed Shabana under her breath.

***

Later that night, as Ted was walking upstairs to his room he could hear a lot of voices coming from the kitchen – Lala jee's was the most prominent. *Should I go?* Ted thought. He decided he should. 'What's all the fuss?' Ted asked once he entered the kitchen. He could see Jamshed, Shyama Prasad, Babu Ram and some ten other odd men huddled up together in front of a transistor.

Lala jee was the first to respond. 'Babu sahib, come sit – I will make you some chai.'

'No Lala jee, that won't be necessary but thank you. What's going on?'

Lala jee smiled and said. 'You know that madman George Fernandes, the President of the Indian Railway Men's Federation, who called a strike on the eighth of this month?'

Ted nodded. 'Yes, I remember – twenty days already? Seems like it's still the first week of May with those massive arrests.'

'Yes, just imagine – so many people will be released and there won't be any more delays for our groceries.'

Ted laughed at Lala jee's comment.

'Sahib, excuse this nutcase, he always dreams about his vegetables and gets concerned about his spices,' Jamshed joined in the conservation.

'All this wouldn't have happened if *she* resigned,' Lala jee teased Jamshed, who was an avid supporter of the Prime Minister.

'Well! Gentlemen, please free to start your political debate – I shall take my leave.' Ted ended up staying there for few more minutes to banter away with Jamshed and Lala jee before leaving for his room.

***

Ted had come a long way from the first day at the office. It was as boring as he'd predicted – the only thing that was a bit different was that there was always someone ready to help him out. An assistant looked after a handful of them, including delivery of tea or a newspaper. There were only a few familiar faces in the offices that Ted was acquainted with from the living quarters. All he wanted was to avoid Cathy's gaze and coming face to face with James, but that was inevitable. Ted soon found out that he would be reporting to James for any offshore visa enquiries. Ted tried his best not to cross paths with him.

That whole afternoon, Ted was busy either introducing himself or being introduced, as well as getting to know the office, the Indian employees and his work, files and papers. He skipped lunch and the files kept mounting on his table.

'Ted, could you come here please?' James called out for Ted at his desk.

'Yes James, what can I do?'

James lifted his eyes from the paper he was deeply engrossed in and he smiled at Ted, handing him some documents. 'If you could look into these and file a report please, that will be great.'

Ted was almost taken back his behaviour. *This is not the same James. Is it?* Ted kept looking at James, standing there astonished.

'Is there anything else you want?' James asked.

Ted shook his head. 'No, thank you.' Ted walked towards his desk absolutely shocked.

***

The office was always Ted's least favourite place, as it took him away from practising poetry with Shabana and kept him in reality. Though Calcutta was an escape, he hated to work. He always looked forward to the evening, to spending time with Shabana and reading poetry together.

When it was five o'clock – time to go home – Ted was still reading files.

'We don't get paid overtime.'

Hearing the familiar voice of James, Ted smiled back at him. 'Oh! It's five already? Thanks James.' Ted was about to get up and shake hands with him but it was too late. James walked away. *What's his problem again?* Ted thought.

Shrugging, he picked up his coat to go when he was interrupted by a tap on his shoulder. He turned back to see a smiling Cathy. His heart sank. 'Hi Cathy, ready to go?'

'Absolutely, can I join you Ted?'

Ted saw that he had no option but to say yes.

On the way to the bungalow, Cathy was quite chatty about how a mother was refused visa as she did not supply enough documents, and how Cathy had faced an abusive man who argued with her because he didn't understand her. Cathy had an endless list of stories that were all about her.

Ted pretended to be interested; he looked away and engaged himself with the moving world. The traffic and the people came as a breath of breath fresh air to him; he now saw the rush hour of people trying to get to a bus and a man narrowly escaping the tram – he was so nonchalant, the man must do that every day and no one cared or was bothered. It seemed like only Ted could see the organised chaos in this part of the world. Ted broke into a smile and came back to Cathy, as if all this while he'd been really interested in what she had to say.

Once in his room, Ted looked at an envelope and a book kept at the side table. Surprised, he picked up the book that was written in Urdu; slowly opening the envelope, he twitched his nose to the smell of jasmine. Ted tried to take the paper carefully but tiny buds of jasmine kept falling off the envelope on the floor. He smiled. The note said, *'Layla and Majnun* for you. I will read it out to you. See you tomorrow. Shabana.'

'Damn! I forgot her *Romeo and Juliet* again,' Ted said aloud. He felt calm, the fatigue of the day wearing off. Ted quickly changed into his tracksuit pants and a loose shirt before heading downstairs. As he approached the kitchen, pacing himself slowly, he screened the kitchen for Shabana.

As he was peddling his way back to his room he crashed into Jamshed, who was carrying an assortment of groceries and herbs in his hands. 'You okay, sahib? Do you need anything?' he asked while bending his knees and trying to manage his balance.

Ted also bent down, picking up the herbs from the floor. 'So sorry Jamshed! Have you seen Shabana?' Ted asked, hoping he sounded innocent.

'Is everything alright, sahib?' Jamshed frowned at him.

Sensing his suspicious tone, Ted quickly changed the topic. 'Oh, is this rosemary?' Ted asked, picking up a sprig of the herb from the floor.

'Yes sahib, we grow this in the garden here for the food and roasts. Also, sometimes we take them home for our use,' Jamshed said smiling. 'But sahib, what do you need Shabana for?'

Hearing the protective fatherly tone from Jamshed, Ted quickly apologised. 'Oh, nothing! So sorry Jamshed, I broke a glass in my room and also needed some tea.'

'Is that all, sahib? You shouldn't have bothered to

come down all the way, you could have just yelled. Lala jee or me could have come.' Jamshed said sympathetically. 'Isn't that so, Lala jee?' Jamshed asked Lala jee, who was just entering the kitchen to prepare the evening meal.

'Absolutely,' Lala jee replied, not knowing what the conversation was about, but obliged to say 'yes' to anything Ted asked on account of Ted liking his French toast. He picked up a few sprigs of rosemary and pointed to Ted. 'Sahib, rusmari for lamb roast tonight.'

Confused, Ted was about to ask Lala jee what he was saying when Shabana walked in the kitchen. Shabana quietly smiled and made herself busy at the kitchen, but that was cut short when Lala jee called for her. 'Shabana, what is that *belaiti dhonepata* called?'

'You mean to say that foreign cilantro, Lala jee?' Shabana asked, pointing at the parsley.

'No! No! Not that. Rusmari.' Lala jee pointed at the sprigs of rosemary.

'Rosemary, Lala jee, not rusmari,' Shabana said, smiling at Lala jee and Ted.

Jamshed, slightly annoyed with the whole scenario, ordered Shabana to go to Ted's room to clear the broken glass and take a pot of tea with her. Ted, relieved to be rescued by Shabana, winked at her, away from the judging eyes of Jamshed and Lala jee, before making his way to the library.

***

'Who is it?' Ted called out at the knock on his door. He waited for a reply but no one replied. *Shabana!*

he thought. Opening the door to a smiling face of Shabana was the best thing that Ted had seen all day. Grabbing the tray from Shabana he carelessly tossed it on the table, spilling tea all over. 'Careful!' Shabana yelled at Ted, placing the broom next to the door.

Ignoring her, Ted grabbed the book of *Romeo and Juliet* that was lying on his bedside table. 'Look what I got for you!' Showing off, Ted flashed the book in front of Shabana.

'Oh, that's really great, Ted. Thank you.' Taking it from his hand, Shabana opened the book to turn a few pages. 'By the way, did you get the book I left in your room of *Layla and Majnun*?'

'I did indeed. So, should we start our lesson in Bangla first?' Ted enquired.

'Oh, Bangla can wait – why don't we read *Layla and Majnun* first? Urdu is better.' Shabana giggled.

'Fair enough. Totally your call ma'am.' Ted saluted at Shabana, which made her laugh. 'Shh!' Ted put his finger to his lips and signalled Shabana to keep her voice down.

Shabana was impressed with Ted's sudden vigilance. 'Shall we then?' Pointing the book at Ted, Shabana made herself comfortable in the chair next to the bed. Shabana turned and read a few pages in Urdu, translating to Ted in English.

> *One night desperate Majnun prayed tearfully,*
> *'Oh Lord of mine who has abandoned me. Why*
> *has Thou 'Majnun' called me? Why hast thou*
> *made a lover of Leila of me? Thou hast made*
> *me a pillow of wild thorns, made me roam day*
> *and night without a home. What dost Thou*
> *want from my imprisonment? Oh Lord of*
> *mine, listen to my plea!'*

The Lord replied, 'Oh lost man, With Layla's love I have your heart filled; The beauty of Layla that you see is just another reflection of Me.'

'That's beautifully explained, Shabana,' Ted praised. 'You make it sound so beautiful, especially when you speak in Urdu. It sounds even better when I can understand in English. This is like an aphrodisiac,' he said cheekily.

'Aphrodisiac – sounds beautiful. What does that even mean?' Shabana asked.

Rolling his eyes, Ted wanted to make sure that he didn't embarrass Shabana. 'Aphrodisiac means … mmm. Let's see, how can I explain? Well, the way you speak Urdu stimulates sexual desires … in me.'

'*Chal*! *Haat*! *Pagla*. Go, move you mad man. You are making a fool of me now.' Shabana giggled, slightly embarrassed.

'No! No! I had no intention to embarrass you. I speak the truth like Majnun.'

They giggled; Shabana felt at ease again. Looking away from Ted she pretended to turn a page from the book; choosing her words carefully, she softly spoke. 'You know what Layla and Majnun mean? Layla means night, like she's a dark beauty – like a wine that intoxicated Majnun, totally absorbing her love. Therefore, Majnun can only mean insane, madly in love.'

Totally mesmerised by the moment, Ted raised her chin towards his face. Shabana had her eyes closed tightly. Ted burst out in laughter. 'Why are you scared?' he asked.

'Scared by your sexual desires.' Shabana popped her eyes open, giggling.

'Shabana!'

The giggles and laughter were cut short with Jamshed calling her name from downstairs. Shabana's face turned white. 'Quickly, break those glasses. Before *Abba* comes up.' Taking two glasses from the table, Ted crashed them on the mosaic floor. There were pieces of glass everywhere. Shabana reached for the top of her blouse – taking a sprig of rosemary out from there, she placed it between the pages of the Layla and Majnun book.

'You use rosemary for a bookmark?' Ted asked surprised.

'You are very observant,' Shabana said, sweeping the glass-riddled floor. There was a knock on his door and this time Shabana looked at Ted, terrified. She signalled Ted to hide the books. Taking both the books from his bed he quickly put them in his drawer.

'Who is it?' Ted enquired.

'Sahib it's me, Jamshed. Is Shabana there?'

'Yes! Yes! She's sweeping the glass off my floor. I have made a real mess, Jamshed. It's very kind of her to help out.' Ted opened the door to let Jamshed in.

Jamshed felt at ease watching Shabana sweep the floor, with her headscarf appropriately resting on her head. 'Sahib, do you know that Shabana is my daughter …' Jamshed paused briefly only to ask Shabana in Bengali how much longer she would take to sweep the glasses. Shabana signalled with her hand: five minutes.

In the meantime Ted pretended to look at Jamshed with surprise. 'Really? I didn't know that.'

Taking advantage of the situation, Jamshed narrated the whole story of how his entire family came to be working here at the bungalow. This time the two men were interrupted by Shabana, who excused herself while taking the pieces of glasses in a bag. 'Shabana, take the pot of tea too,' Jamshed snarled at Shabana.

'Oh, I haven't finished the tea yet. Maybe later,' Ted interrupted.

'As you say. Is there anything else sahib?' Jamshed asked politely.

'No not at all Jamshed – I better rest with a cup of tea and we can continue on your story next time we meet. Shabana, you can come later to collect the pot of tea.' Ted smiled at both of them.

Ordering Shabana to go down, Jamshed then turned to Ted, saying, 'Sahib, when you are done with the tea simply put the pot outside your room, it will be collected later.'

'Of course,' Ted replied, disappointed.

Closing the door behind him, Ted opened the drawer. He took the book of Layla and Majnun, carefully picking the sprig of rosemary from between the pages and holding it to his nose – he tried to hold on to the lingering smell of Shabana.

***

The dinner table was filled with diners and as usual Ted was late. 'Look, babu sahib is here. The politician's son.' James left no sarcasm in taunting Ted.

What's his problem? Ted thought. Pulling up a chair behind him, he sat next to James and looked at him with a smile while the servants haggled in front of Ted with plates and other condiments.

'Babu sahib, what would you like – continental or Indian dinner?' One of the servants asked Ted.

'What's on the continental menu?' Ted asked.

'Australian lamb roast and potato salad with English pudding. He will like it. Won't you Ted?' James replied on his behalf to the servant.

By now Ted was getting quite anxious with this bipolar behaviour. A person so approachable in office and yet so ruthless elsewhere. Ted sat quietly, not retaliating at all. 'Babu sahib, your dinner,' the servant said, handing him the plate. The aroma of rosemary and lamb was enough for Ted to quickly forget James. Taking his knife and fork he cut through the tough piece of lamb and placed a forkful of the meat to his mouth. The lamb was tough. Ted didn't mind at all but he was rudely nudged by James, who looked at him, laughing. 'I told you that you'd find the lamb entertaining.'

That's it. Ted put his fork down and looked straight at James. 'What's your problem, mate? Why the hell are you rude to me?'

Taking a sip of water from his glass, James pushed his plate back and looked straight at Ted. 'Ask your father about James Sullivan.' Throwing his napkin in Ted's face, James walked away. Shocked by all this, the whole dining hall came to a standstill.

'Come on, show's over!' Ted yelled and returned to his plate. He knew his appetite was gone but if he left the dining hall now he would look like a coward.

He was fighting with these thoughts just as Cathy sat next to him to add fire to the fury. 'You should not let him speak to you like that,' Cathy protested.

'If you don't mind, Cathy, I would like to finish my dinner in peace and go to my room,' Ted said with his head down, pretending to eat.

'Sure, I understand, but what has James got to do with your father?' Cathy still sounded persistent.

Looking at Cathy in disgust, Ted pushed his plate and walked away.

'Te … Ted, your dinner?' Cathy screamed from behind.

Ted ran straight to his room upstairs and placed a trunk call to Melbourne. Before it connected he hung up and decided to wait until the morning to digest the situation.

***

Dorothy drew her car to a halt at the traffic lights. It was a sunny day in Melbourne; the warm winter sun glaring on the car's windscreen just felt quite the right thing for her at that moment. Her eyes drowsy with sleep, she blinked heavily. She put her head down on the steering wheel and closed her eyes for a few seconds, ignoring the horns going mad behind her.

She woke to a sudden knock on her window. 'You okay ma'am? Do you need me to call you an ambulance? You seemed to have caused chaos with the traffic.' The young cop smiled at her.

Dorothy, feeling a bit embarrassed, managed to say, 'It was only for a few seconds until the lights changed. How long I have been like this, officer?'

'It's been around 20 minutes. Can I have your license, ma'am?' the cop asked.

Running through her bag, Dorothy reached for her wallet. Handing the license to the young cop, she noticed another cop was busy diverting traffic the other way. She looked behind her to see the chaos she'd created on Bell Street. The cop took her license to his patrol car and ran a few checks; he was quick to return with some breath analyser. It read nil for her alcohol count. Knowing who she was, he signalled the other officer who was sitting in the patrol car to come to him. 'Ma'am, sometimes stress can bring this out in lots of our motorists. I'll have Constable Stevenson escort you to your home. I will be right behind you,' the young cop said with a smile.

'Absolutely. Whatever you think is best, officer,' Dorothy replied, very embarrassed. *What was I thinking? I should try to stop making more work for John*, Dorothy thought. The toll of John's political campaign was already tiring her out but she wanted the legacy of her late father-in-law Richard Smith to succeed. The hunger of power was so deep-seated in her that she didn't care if her husband, or anyone for that matter, wanted what she wanted. It was all about Dorothy and John Smith's political career – an ambition she wanted to fulfil at any cost.

She took a left turn towards Flinders Street Station and onto St Kilda Road, making a quick turn towards Toorak. She was very cautious with the speed as the officer was sitting next to her. She tried to strike up a conversation with the young officer to show her gratitude. 'So Mr Stevenson, how long have you been in the police force?' Dorothy asked while checking her rear view mirror – the cop car was right behind her.

'Just three months, ma'am. I am still training,' Constable Stevenson replied.

'We need officers like you to make us feel protected.' Dorothy could see the young constable blush with her comment. 'How old are you?'

'Twenty, ma'am,' Constable Stevenson replied.

Dorothy smiled. 'I have a son who is twenty-four – he is in India, works at the foreign office for the Australian Consulate.' Dorothy's voice softened. Suddenly she missed Ted and everything that was attached to him. She wanted to hear his voice again and continued the rest of the trip in silence.

As she entered into South Yarra she drove past the train station and into Chapel Street, turning towards Glenferrie Road – towards home.

'Thank you, Constable – lovely to chat with you and good luck with your training,' Dorothy said.

'Thank you ma'am!'

The officer from the patrol car came out to shake hands with Dorothy and to check if she was okay for one last time. 'I hope you are feeling better and good luck with the campaign, ma'am.'

Dorothy smiled and assured the officer that she was absolutely fine. She walked straight inside the main entrance of their Toorak mansion. She looked at the huge clock that was hung in the hallway: it showed 2.35 pm. 'Gee whiz, I'm late!' Dorothy cursed under her breath. 'Maria, could you please bring me some coffee?' she screamed out to her housekeeper while passing the kitchen towards the lounge. Taking her diary out, she placed a call to Ted.

'Mother! Thank you for calling back.'

'Sorry I couldn't talk properly before. What's the matter Ted, is everything alright?' Dorothy asked while making herself comfortable in the sofa.

'Absolutely. No, no, you're not late. Actually, I wanted to talk to Dad. It seems like he has upset someone here. Does James Sullivan ring a bell?'

Dorothy paused; looking outside at the courtyard, she took a deep breath. 'What is he doing there?' Dorothy asked.

Ted narrated the whole story to her. Dorothy was about to reply when Maria brought in some coffee. As she was about to pour Dorothy a cup from the pot, Dorothy signalled for her to leave the lounge for some privacy. 'Well … it's time that your father spoke about James Sullivan to you.'

'What do you mean, Mother?'

'I cannot answer that at the moment – I need to discuss this with your father first. Could I call you tomorrow?'

'No Mother – I need to talk to him today.' Ted sounded agitated and demanding.

Dorothy didn't want to aggravate the stress in her son's voice. 'He's not home yet, he's at a golf club discussing his campaign.'

'Doesn't matter Mother – I am not going to work. As soon as he comes just call me.' Ted hung up; for the first time in his life he was firm with Dorothy and he didn't say goodbye.

Dorothy was now more concerned about her son than before and she could foresee a storm brewing up in their lives – the name James Sullivan was enough to lose her bearings. Usually nothing frazzled Dorothy Smith, but today she didn't know what to do.

***

John Smith walked in, interrupting Dorothy from her thoughts. 'Darling, I am back … oh! Nice coffee for both of us?' He eyed the tray with the pot of coffee, biscuits and cakes that had been untouched since Maria left it for Dorothy a couple of hours ago. John reached for a shortbread cookie, at the same time placing a quick kiss on Dorothy's cheek. Realising that she didn't respond to his kiss with the usual enthusiasm, he asked, 'What's the matter darling?'

Dorothy poured herself some coffee, realising it had gone cold. She yelled for Maria to get them some fresh coffee and bring hers to the courtyard, giving her husband some space.

John quickly finished the rest of the cookie and stopped Dorothy. 'What's the matter? What's going on?'

'You need to call Ted right now.' Dorothy sounded angry.

'Why? You are sounding pretty tense. I will call tomorrow – he will be …' John paused to look at his watch. 'Being four and a half hours behind, he must be on his way to his office.'

'John, call him today – he has not gone to the office.'

***

'Morning, Dad. I tried to talk to you earlier,' Ted began, taking a deep breath.

'Yeah, I was out playing golf and working on the campaign. What's the matter?' Ted was not his usual self; he didn't ask about golf or about his campaign – he seemed detached.

'Dad, I have come across this guy – extremely rude, and sadly he's also my team leader in the office. I have no qualms with him in the office, but he doesn't spare one moment to insult me whenever we sit down at the dining hall. Any given chance he humiliates me for being a politician's son in front of other diners, always talking to me in a very passive aggressive tone. Last night he asked me to ask you about him. Do you know James Sullivan?'

John froze. His cheeks went red and he could feel the heat on his face. For a few seconds there was an awkward silence over the phone, as if the line had gone dead.

'Dad, are you there?'

'Yes, I'm here,' John finally spoke. He sat down looking at Dorothy outside, who had her back to him in the courtyard. 'It's about time you knew about James Sullivan. I did not want you to find out about him like this … but then, will another time matter? James Sullivan is your half-brother, my illegitimate son.'

The only thing that John heard was his own breathing over the phone. Ted broke the awkward silence between the two. 'What do you mean, Dad? Is it really true? Does Mum know about it? When were you planning to tell me?'

'Calm down, Ted. Your mum knows about James and we were not planning to tell you at all because everything has been dealt with. There is nothing more to say.' John sounded firm, as if he wasn't interested at all.

'I want to know, Dad – everything. Please, you owe me this.' Ted sounded persistent and helpless.

Sensing his son's anxiety, John Smith had no choice. He poured himself a coffee from the pot Maria had just left for him. Like a defeated man, he hung his head while wiping a tear. 'It was around 1946–47 … things were very different then. I was on a campaign with your grandfather in central Queensland and Tina, James's mother, was working as an intern in the office. One night after a party we both were drunk and … we were young. Honestly, we didn't know what was happening.' John paused for a while, waiting for Ted to say something – but there was nothing, not even Ted breathing into the phone. 'Are you there?' John asked.

Clearing his voice, Ted found the courage to say the inevitable. 'So! You both fucked up and she raised a bastard that I come to know halfway across the world. How do you justify that?'

'Don't be so harsh, son. Yes, we had a one-night stand and your grandfather became very angry and fired Tina.' John took a sip of his coffee. 'I was already with your mother and she was the one I wanted to marry, so we paid off Tina and did everything for James. He was never to find out who his biological father is.'

'I have nothing to say to you, Father – just that I am very disappointed in you and Mum.' Ted hung up.

John Smith put the receiver down and walked up to Dorothy in the courtyard, putting his arm across her shoulders. A teardrop fell into Dorothy's neck; it felt as if John was waiting for this wound to heal. She turned to face him. 'I told Ted, Dorothy … I told him. He is angry.' John started sobbing.

Dorothy did not say anything; instead, she took John in her arms and comforted him like a little baby. 'It's going to be okay, John. You need to understand that it's been our big secret for twenty-six years and he will need time. Darling, you need to get a hold of yourself,' said Dorothy.

'I didn't want Ted to find out like this. Why would James do that? He never had to know in the first place who his father is,' John questioned himself.

Hearing her husband's predicament, Dorothy had to quickly take matters into her hands and stop John's whining. Taking his hands in hers, Dorothy looked straight into John's eyes. 'What's done is done – we cannot turn back time and make everything go away. This way or that way, it doesn't matter anymore. He knows it now. Give him time. We cannot chase James or Tina for this. We have to be careful; your election campaign is at stake. Let me handle Ted and ask him to persuade James not to spread the scandal around.' Dorothy sounded firm and cold.

John bent down on his knees – the grass underneath felt blissful – and grabbed Dorothy with both hands, laying his head on her waist while continuing to sob. 'Save me from this mess.'

Looking at her helpless husband, she didn't say anything anymore to sound empathetic; instead she looked down on John, caressing his hair.

***

Ted hung up on his father without saying goodbye. He felt betrayed. *How could they?* he thought. He wanted to go back to the office and hit James. He hit his hand against the wall. 'That hurt!' he said to himself, kicking the chair in front of him. His body was overcome with fatigue.

In a foetal positon, he fell asleep on the floor. When he got up it was dark already. 'How long have I been sleeping for?' he said to himself, as if he'd woken from a bad dream.

Just as his mixed emotions were spurring him to lash out again, he heard a knock on the door. 'Who is it?' Ted asked. There was no answer. It must be Shabana. He closed his eyes for a split second. He wanted to be alone; he didn't want anyone around. He switched on his light to see the time, then turned the light off again, not responding to the door knock; instead he went to bed to bury himself in grief. He could see the shadow behind the door still lurking, and he felt sad as he wanted to see Shabana – but tonight was not the night for Urdu poetry and English literature.

Just as Ted was about to close his eyes, he noticed something whisked under his door and the shadow slowly disappearing. He got up from his bed and turned on the light. He bent down to pick up a piece of folded paper, opening it to see something written in Urdu with a sprig of rosemary. He took the piece of rosemary to his nose and everything that was connected with Shabana made him feel at ease. He did not know what it was: the calming smell of Rosemary or the message in Urdu. He turned the page to see an English translation: 'You talk when you cease to be at peace with your thoughts.'

Ted rushed to open the door to see if Shabana was still there. *Is it too late?* Ted thought. The hallway outside was dim and the light from his room was the only thing that made it possible for him to search the corners of the stairs. Something moved that made Ted shift his attention to the corner of the door. 'Shabana, is that you?' Ted whispered. There was no response. 'Shabana!' This time Ted called out a little louder.

'Shhh! I am here. Keep your voice down,' Shabana called out from inside his room.

Ted ran inside, locking the door behind him. 'I'm sorry I didn't open sooner. It has been quite a day for me.' Ted walked closer to Shabana; in his hand he had the sprig of rosemary. 'Who wrote that and what did it mean, Shabana?' Taking her hand as they sat on the floor, Ted looked straight into her big brown eyes.

'It's by a Lebanese poet, Khalil Gibran, from his book of poetry *The Prophet*. You looked disturbed so I ...'

Shabana was quickly interrupted by Ted as he put his finger on her lips. 'Shhh! Just read me the rest and sit with me.'

Shabana could sense he was not the same Ted today. Without hesitation she continued. *'You talk when you cease to be at peace with your thoughts; And when you can no longer dwell in the solitude of your heart you live in your lips and sound is a diversion and a pastime. And in much of your talking, thinking is half-murdered.'*

There was absolute silence when Shabana finished reciting the poem. Slowly Ted lay his head on her lap, closing his eyes. 'Do you think living in the past is a waste of time?'

Shabana did not know what he was implying, but she had seen it all at the dinner table with James. Choosing her words carefully, she rubbed her fingers through Ted's hair. 'The past just makes a lot of sound. When there is no peace in your heart you begin to respond to that sound – you get agitated and you fight to make it go away. But it's best to forget and move on.' When Ted began to sob, Shabana quickly bent down, cupping his face and rubbing his tears. 'What is the matter, *janemaan* (sweetheart)?'

'Shabana, what if I told you that Calcutta is now burning inside me like one of those Hindu bodies that burn non-stop in those crematoriums – I want to get out of here, but if I go, in Melbourne I will be completely burnt.' Ted looked at her with wet eyes.

'I still don't understand Ted. Don't speak in riddles, tell me openly,' Shabana requested.

'James is my half-brother – one of my father's dirty secrets.' Ted looked away from Shabana, embarrassed and crying.

There was a brief silence and then Shabana slowly moved her hands towards Ted, picking him up from the floor and guiding him towards the bed. 'Come lie down, you will feel better. I am next to you,' Shabana said, running her fingers through his hair.

Ted looked at her, slowly raising his head; they hesitated for a moment. Ted tried to look away but Shabana, gently stroking his face, sealed her lips with his in a soft kiss. Ted was overcome with emotion; he teased her tongue, slowly manipulating his way past her lips – he finally kissed her passionately. Shabana broke free and placed her finger on Ted's lips, smiling at him as she removed her kameez shirt.

Slowly unbuttoning Ted's shirt at the same time, she placed her head on his bare chest. Grabbing her hair from the back, Ted kissed her once again, taking charge. Taking the rest of her clothing off, she placed her naked body on top of his. Rubbing her fingers on his cheeks, she took them gently to her lips.

'Are you sure about this, darling?' Ted asked Shabana, stroking her hair gently.

Withdrawing herself from Ted, Shabana positioned herself carefully on top of Ted, pointing a finger on Ted's lips. '*Janemaan*, I am sure about you.' Taking his hands, she guided them to her naked body.

Ted was spellbound by her invitation; he couldn't resist flipping Shabana underneath him, kissing her. They made love throughout the night.

***

'*Janemaan*, does your heartbeat always go fast like this?' Shabana laughed, teasing Ted with a sprig of rosemary while her head rested on Ted's chest.

With a pinch on his nose, Ted stopped Shabana from tickling him again with the rosemary. 'What's with you and this sprig of herb?' Ted asked, carefully taking it out of her hand.

'You have no idea how important it is to us, for sickness. The hakim gives it to us for the common cold and lots of other medications: hair loss, dandruff and also for calming the senses,' Shabana said with slight annoyance while getting out of bed.

'Why are you getting angry? I'm just surprised that this day and age you believe in a witch doctor. It's the 70s, missy,' Ted teased, grabbing Shabana's wrist. 'Where are you going?' He tried to pull Shabana closer to him.

'I have to go, Ted. Soon it will be morning and everyone will come looking for me. They think that I have been helping Lala jee all night, cleaning the kitchen,' Shabana said softly, kissing Ted's hands.

'I think I love you,' Ted said aloud.

'I know, *janemaan*,' Shabana said while dressing. She sat next to Ted, kissing his forehead. '*Janemaan*, you know that you and me … is not possible in this lifetime. I am already engaged to someone and although it means nothing to me … what we had last night was special but we should not complicate that. We know sometimes some things are not possible.'

Ted kissed Shabana's hand. 'When were you planning to tell me about your engagement?' he asked, now understanding why she wore a ring in a chain across her neck.

'Never! Also, you never asked. But I had to tell you this today, because we both know how we feel about each other … and you will not stop me,' Shabana replied.

Ted pulled Shabana towards him and embraced her. They both were in each other's arms in absolute silence. Shabana buried her face in Ted's chest and all she could hear was his heart beating. Finally!

Ted broke the silence. '*My bounty is as boundless as the sea, my love as deep; the more I give to thee, the more I have, for both are infinite.*'

Shabana looked at Ted with foggy eyes. '*Romeo and Juliet.* Don't make it difficult for me, *janemaan*,' Shabana said.

Ted looked away from her. He said scathingly, 'I'm falling in love with you but I hate this. I can't tell anyone – so don't you dare cry, as you will now go back to a man you don't love. You will be with this man every night, making love to him.' Ted turned to see Shabana – by now her eyes almost foggy with tears. 'Please don't look at me like that. You know me, I'll never be able to let go of you … I will dream to make it possible.'

Shabana ran to him and threw her arms around his neck, softly whispering, 'We will have each other, I promise you *janemaan*, in another life or in *Jannat* – paradise – we will be together. I know now it's difficult but it's best this way.'

'Then don't cry and make me weak,' Ted said while wiping her tears. 'Yesterday my parents betrayed me and today you are betraying me of the love I need,' Ted sneered.

'Don't be so cruel to yourself … guilt doesn't get anyone anywhere. So, stop pitying yourself. Love is there – it just cannot be justified,' Shabana scolded Ted.

Ted nodded, looked at the ground beneath him for few seconds and then said something that took Shabana by surprise: 'I am sorry.'

'What for? Being you? Oh, my *pagla firang* (mad white man), emotions are running high. Don't be sorry, my *janemaan*,' Shabana said with a laugh.

'Don't go. When will you be back?' Ted begged.

'If you let me go then I will be back. You have to let people go to come back, you know,' Shabana teased.

'Did I stop you?' Ted chuckled.

Gobsmacked by the quick response from Ted, Shabana rolled her eyes and ran for the door, before quickly turning back to kiss Ted and whisper in his ears, 'Also, my hakim is not a witch doctor.'

Ted laughed. 'Go! Before I grab you and stop you.'

***

Cathy was softly breaking into tears as she saw Shabana walking down the stairs from Ted's room. *She must've been there the whole night – it's four in the morning,* Cathy thought. Rubbing tears from her eyes she felt angry and disgusted by the thought. *How could Ted like the help's daughter – how could he?*

Closing the door behind her, she stomped up and down the room. She wanted to scream, to bring the entire complex down and tell everyone about them. 'Ted is mine, Shabana, how could you … you foreign bitch,' Cathy muttered under her breath. She opened the window to get some fresh air; it was as if the city lights were talking to her. Cathy's eyes were shining like the city lights and suddenly she smiled. 'Ted, you will pay for this … for that whore.' She smiled while wiping her tears.

Her eyes fixed on an advertisement. It said, 'Call Australia Education Centre to study in Australia.' *No! I cannot do that! Who will believe me? It's a stupid idea,* Cathy thought. She pressed her head against the window and saw the milkman delivering the morning milk. Lala jee walked up to the courtyard and then there was a man behind him walking towards the gate – it was Jamshed getting ready for *wudu* for his morning *namaz* (prayers). Cathy quickly put on her dressing gown and slippers and rushed downstairs.

'Good Morning Jamshed, do you have a moment?' Cathy asked a surprised Jamshed.

'Is everything alright Memsahib, do you need anything?'

'Everything's okay … I just wanted to speak to you urgently on a very important matter,' Cathy persisted.

Jamshed looked at her blankly.

***

'Who is it?' James called out, hearing the knock on his door.

'It's me, Ted.'

There was a brief pause. 'What do you want?' James asked, reluctant to open the door.

'I just want to have a quick word with you, I won't be long,' Ted replied politely.

James opened the door with a grim look on his face. 'Make it quick,' James replied, signalling Ted to come in.

'I don't know what's appropriate to say or do but can I just say, I am sorry for my father's actions,' Ted said with his head down.

James looked at him with a frown. 'Do you think that by you saying sorry, it will change everything?'

Ted looked at him and said, 'No, it will not … but I hope to put my hand forward in friendship.' Ted extended his hand to James.

James laughed out loud. 'Are you serious, man? After all your father has done to me, you think coming here, apologising to me, will make it all right? Fuck! Man, what courage,' James mocked Ted.

'I am deeply sorry, James – think about me for once and what I must have gone through when they told me the truth about you. A thousand miles from home I come to know about my half-brother,' Ted said politely.

'Do you think I give a fuck?' James said, showing Ted the door.

'Before I leave, all I will say is that from the bottom of my heart, I am sorry.' Ted paused. 'Also, I'll be taking a few days off. I will send you my leave application.' Ted walked out the door.

The door slammed behind Ted with a bang, but to his surprise he didn't feel suffocated or despised anymore. He felt lighter and contained.

Ted walked outside to the courtyard to catch some fresh air of peace, when he saw Jamshed walking straight towards him. *Oh! Does he know about me and Shabana already? No, how would he?* he thought. He quickly put up a smile for Jamshed.

'Good day babu sahib – you look happy,' Jamshed said in a very professional tone.

'I am, Jamshed, I've taken a few days off, so very happy. Before you go, where can I find the perfume market in Calcutta?'

Jamshed frowned at Ted's odd request. 'You mean the Itar bazaar?' Jamshed asked. Ted looked back at him, confused. 'Oh, sorry to confuse you. In Bengali *itar* means perfume. It's in Baro Bazaar,' Jamshed replied.

'Is any car free today?' Ted asked Jamshed.

'There is one, our car for the grocery. I will tell him to take you,' Jamshed replied.

'That's great,' Ted said, hugging Jamshed.

'Ahem! Sahib.' Realising that he hugged Jamshed too tightly, Ted immediately released Jamshed and walked towards the waiting car. '*Pagla firang* (mad white man),' Jamshed cursed under his breath, not laughing this time.

*****

There were three knocks at the door. Ted quietly opened the door to see a smiling Shabana standing there, pretending to serve tea to Ted. 'Sahib, your tea,' Shabana said to a smiling Ted.

Quickly entering his room, Ted grabbed the pot from her hand and tossed it to the table carelessly, spilling tea everywhere. He grabbed Shabana and pulled her closer to him, kissing her passionately. 'Close your eyes,' Ted requested.

'Why?' Shabana asked.

'Come on, close your eyes. Please,' Ted pleaded with his hands folded.

Shabana nodded at Ted's sincere request and closed her eyes. Ted put in front of her a purple glass bottle with a gold cap. The bottle had intricate glass carving. Ted opened the cap and put the bottle in front of Shabana's nose. 'Take a deep breath and smell this.'

Shabana inhaled and exhaled quickly next to the bottle. Her lips broke into a smile. '*Janemaan*! It's rosemary.' She opened her eyes and grabbed the bottle. 'Oh! It's beautiful. Where did you get this?'

'Actually, it's pretty funny. I asked your father. He said Baro Bazaar,' Ted replied, laughing.

'*Abba*? That would be interesting. Why did you get me a gift?'

'You love the herb and I wanted to give you something that you love. Consider it as my wedding present,' Ted mocked.

'Do you have to bring that up?' Shabana grumbled, handing the bottle back to Ted.

'Sorry,' Ted replied. 'I also went and apologised to James. I did it to feel better – I did it for myself.'

'You are happy now?' Shabana asked, taking the bottle back from him and smelling it.

'I think so,' Ted replied.

Taking Ted's hand, she leaned forward to kiss him on his lips. 'Thank you for this lovely gift,' she said, sitting on the floor cross-legged. Ted joined her, resting his head on her thighs. Shabana carefully poured a drop of the perfume and massaged it on Ted's head.

'That is so relaxing. Read me something – but how much time do we have?' Ted asked.

'Hmm, an hour. Okay, how about Rumi?' Shabana asked Ted.

'It's your call. Anything,' Ted replied.

Clearing her voice, Shabana began reciting:

> *Stay close, my heart, to the one who knows your ways;*

> *Come into the shade of the tree that always has fresh flowers.*

> *Don't stroll idly through the bazaar of the perfume markers;*

Stay in the shop of the sugar-seller.

If you don't find true balance, anyone can deceive you;

Anyone can trick out of a thing of straw,

And make you take it for gold.

'That's beautiful.' Ted said.

'I know – for you, *janemaan*. Look at you – you took me for gold.' Shabana smirked.

'I am happy for you to deceive me,' Ted said with a laugh, grabbing her and pushing her down on the floor, kissing her as they made passionate love.

September–October 1974

AT THE BREAKFAST TABLE, everyone was quiet; it was as if everything was in slow motion. It had been almost six months since Ted had come to India and two since he found out James was his half-brother. Everything was normal except for one thing: Cathy was unusually quiet. 'Morning Cathy! How have you been?' Ted asked, making himself comfortable in the seat opposite to her.

'I am fine thanks.' Cathy sounded cold.

'I haven't seen you for ages,' Ted replied, taken aback by Cathy's short response.

'I was always here – you seem to be lost these days,' Cathy replied rudely.

'What's with the tone, Cath?' Ted asked, surprised.

'You will find out,' Cathy replied, walking away from the breakfast table.

Shabana was watching all this near the door. She looked at Ted and quizzed him with her face. Ted shrugged at Shabana, throwing his hands up in the air. She smiled sweetly, and they stared at each other for a moment without concern.

Jamshed, who was walking inside the dining area, saw the exchange of looks between the two. Ted noticed this and tried to warn Shabana, who was totally unaware of this – but it was too late. Jamshed walked straight towards Shabana. 'What's all this happening, Shabana?'

Seeing her father in a rage she managed politely, 'What happened, *Abba*?'

'Get out of here now and go home, before I raise my hand in front of all these people,' Jamshed whispered to her angrily. Slowly getting the gist of the entire situation, Shabana did not hesitate – she left the room quickly. Jamshed looked back at Ted with the same rage which he saw Shabana.

Ted was now nervous, both of what Jamshed might do to him and about Shabana. *What's happening today?* Ted thought. It was hard to digest it all.

Across the table from him, James was sipping his coffee as he watched.

***

'Shabana! Shabana! Where the hell are you? You wretched girl.' Jamshed stormed inside the house, looking for her like a raging bull.

'What's the matter? Why are you so mad?' Mumtaz asked.

'Where is she?'

'Inside in the kitchen,' Mumtaz replied nervously.

Shabana was making rotis for the evening meal; her back was facing Jamshed as he walked in. She was calm. 'Come *Abba*, I have made some fresh rotis – let me serve you with *sabzi* (mixed vegetables).'

His daughter's peaceful nature agitated Jamshed even more. He grabbed Shabana's plaited hair and dragged her towards the main room. 'What's going on with you and that *firang*?' Jamshed demanded.

'*Abba*! You are hurting me,' Shabana pleaded.

'Hurting you? What do you know about hurting? You have no idea, what you did was even more than hurt. With that *kaffir* infidel.' He pushed Shabana to the ground and rushed to the kitchen to get a burning piece of wood from the hearth. 'Today I can believe it all as I saw with my own eyes. My own daughter.' Jamshed was seething

'No!' Mumtaz cried. 'Jamshed, for Allah's sake, it's your daughter.'

Jamshed pushed Mumtaz to one side and raged towards Shabana with the burning piece of wood. 'Now will you stop meeting that infidel?' Jamshed pulled Shabana's hair towards the burning wood.

'Do whatever you have to do – I will not reply to that.'

That angered Jamshed even more. Shabana knew what was coming next. She closed her eyes. Jamshed pushed her to the floor and placed the burning hot wood on her right foot. Shabana screamed in pain.

'That will stop you from going,' Jamshed screamed at her. 'Mumtaz, call the hakim now and get her ready for the *nikkah* with Salman tomorrow. I have arranged everything.' Jamshed threw the remainder of the burning piece of wood back in the hearth and stormed out of the house.

Mumtaz ran towards Shabana and embraced her. 'Let me get the hakim for you. Razia, Razia, where are you?' Mumtaz screamed.

'Coming *Aami* (Mother),' Razia replied, running towards them in the main room. What Razia saw was hard for her to digest.

Mumtaz had to nudge Razia. 'Razia, go now, get the hakim.' Mumtaz then quickly dashed to the bathroom to fill a plastic tub with cold water from the storage tank. When she came to the main room, Shabana was already unconscious. Fearing the worst, she sprinkled some cold water on Shabana's face. Shabana was slowly coming to her senses, to Mumtaz's relief. She dipped Shabana's right foot into the cold tub and waited for the hakim to come. 'Is it a little better now?'

Shabana nodded.

'*Beti* (daughter), do as your father says, otherwise things will only get worse for all of us. There is no future with the *firang*. Cathy memsahib ...' Mumtaz stopped, realising what she was about to say was not required.

'*Aami*, why did you stop? How did *Abba* know about all this?' Mumtaz looked away from Shabana. '*Aami*, you are hiding something, please tell me,' Shabana pleaded with her hands folded.

'The firangi ... in the living quarters ... Cathy memsahib ... Your abba has known for quite some time now,' Mumtaz said reluctantly.

'What?' Shabana screamed, shocked. *How did she know about us?* she thought.

Her thoughts were interrupted by Razia and the hakim. The hakim examined her foot, applied some turmeric paste and bandaged it; he also asked Mumtaz to give her *phitkari* (alum mixed with milk). 'Mumtaz bi, she will be able to use her right foot in no time. She is fine. If she's stressed, just rub some rosemary oil on her head. She will feel relaxed.' The hakim smiled at Shabana. 'By the way, what happened, Mumtaz bi?'

Mumtaz was about to say something when Shabana interrupted. 'Hakim jee, I didn't realise while cooking that the piece of wood was out and I put my foot there by mistake.'

The hakim was not convinced, but smiled at Shabana and said, 'Yes, these days even pieces of wood seem to have their own feet! Anyhow, do as I say and you will be okay in no time.'

Shabana waited for Mumtaz to pay the hakim and show him to the door. '*Aami*, let me go to Ted one last time … I must meet him, please. He needs me. Please, *Aami*. I beg you.' Shabana got up to walk towards the door.

'Have you gone mad, Shabana? If your *abba* finds out, he will kill both of us. Just let the *firang* be safe too. Your *abba* spared him because he is in the foreign office and tomorrow is your wedding.' Mumtaz was now adamant in her tone. 'This is it – stay here.'

***

Ted paced up and down his room, waiting to hear from Shabana. He looked at his watch: it was 8.00 pm and he hadn't seen Shabana all day, even at dinner. Jamshed was also missing. *Hope she is okay,* he thought and was about to pour himself a glass of water when he heard a knock on his door. *Shabana?* Ted rushed to open the door. 'Mother!' Ted looked at her shocked. 'What are you doing here?'

'Won't you ask your mother to come inside?' Dorothy replied.

'Of course. Please come in,' Ted requested.

'Well, we never had a chat about your dad and James … and I really missed you, Ted,' Dorothy said while making herself comfortable on the bed. She looked at her surroundings and was appalled by it all. 'Everything in Melbourne awaits you, dear – what are you doing in this godforsaken place?'

Ted was looking at his mother very closely now. 'Mother, why exactly are you here?'

'I told you,' Dorothy replied.

'Seriously, Mother?' Ted waited for an explanation.

'I am here for you – to save you from the hands of a maid, for crying out loud. What were you thinking, Ted?' Dorothy screamed. 'How could you? First your father and now you – we cannot afford to have a scandal right now.'

'Mother! How can you? Who told you that?' Ted screamed back at her.

Dorothy raised her voice in anger. 'Oh, shut up! I am tired of both you and your father. Tired of clearing your mess. Tired of handling such weak men. Look, I am here to take you with me. I have settled everything with your dad – he will speak to the foreign office and transfer you to Canberra.'

'How dare you, Mother? How dare you?' Ted rebelled.

'I dare because there are consequences to your actions. You are an educated man, do you want to be with someone who thinks a cow and an elephant god is something to worship? Seriously, son?' Dorothy's voice softened but was still firm.

'Mother, stop calling her a maid … and it's people's faith, you cannot be judgemental about that. And she is not Hindu, she's Muslim. I never saw her religion or her occupation. I like her because of who she is, not because of what she could have been!' Ted screamed.

'Son, it's no use – you should prepare yourself to go back to Australia. Ted, listen to me, there's a whole life in front of you – you will meet hundreds of women, but that doesn't mean you have to give your heart to everyone. If it wasn't for your friend, colleague … I don't know but whoever, a well-wisher, I wouldn't have come here. Your father is a political figure now – I cannot take any risk. I thought it was impossible for my Teddy to fall in love with a maid here. You are despicable.'

'Mother, get out! Get out now!' Ted yelled at Dorothy.

There was a brief silence, then Dorothy slowly walked towards the door and stopped to look at Ted. 'I did what any mother would do to save her son's life. Think. Here is a ticket for you to return to Melbourne.'

Ted walked straight towards her, taking the ticket in her hand and tearing it in two. 'This is my answer and you can leave now before I forget who you are.' Tears were building up in his eyes.

Dorothy heard the door slam behind her as she left.

Behind closed doors Ted couldn't understand who could have been the informer to his mother. He so wanted to know how Shabana was.

***

'Shabana Ali, daughter of Jamshed Ali, son of Nizam Ali, do you agree to this wedding with the *meher* of fifty thousand rupees? Do you accept this marriage to Salman Qureshi, son of Junaid Qureshi son of Saif Querishi?'

'*Qubool hai* (I accept),' Shabana replied.

'Congratulations! Jamshed and Mumtaz, from today Shabana is ours! She now belongs to this house – my granddaughter in-law,' Mumtaz's mother declared again, screaming with joy.

Jamshed was finally happy, seeing Shabana wed to Mumtaz's brother's son. There were firecrackers bursting outside and the celebrations continued late into the night.

The next day, Shabana left for Salman's house. She was like a dead woman walking, limping on one foot; all she held in her hand was the perfume bottle Ted gave her. She did not cry or bid her goodbyes.

'What happened to her foot?' Salman's mother asked Mumtaz.

'Oh, nothing, she was cooking and she didn't see one of the wood pieces came out of the hearth – she stepped on it by accident.' Mumtaz maintained Shabana's version. Salman's mother looked shocked.

***

Shabana's new home didn't make any difference. She wanted to see Ted just once to see if he was okay, because she knew he was not strong. Most importantly, Ted didn't even know she was now married. She knew that her life was now with Salman – as his wife – and it would be the end of her love story with Ted.

Shabana sat in her bedroom, which was overly decorated with maroon velvet drapes and furniture. The bed she sat on had an elaborate gold and green embroidered bedspread. She hated every bit of it and the room felt quite stuffy. She took out the perfume bottle from her bag and took a deep breath, inhaling the rosemary scent. Her head swung from one side to the other and she collapsed on the floor; the bottle broke in tiny little pieces with the rosemary perfume spilling on the floor.

Shabana lay there unconscious on the floor for a good five minutes until Salman noticed her. '*Aami*, come quickly, Shabana is unconscious here,' Salman screamed out. Salman's mother and grandmother both came into the room. 'What's that potent smell?' Salman asked himself.

'Can someone call the hakim?' Shabana's grandmother yelled.

Salman ran out to fetch their family doctor instead for his newly married bride.

By the time the doctor came around, Shabana was awake and people were huddled around her. The doctor checked her temperature and then her pulse. He smiled. 'Nothing to worry about, all okay. Needs rest.' The doctor collected his bag and called Salman to come outside with him. 'Your wife needs a check-up. It could be stress, could be hormonal. Bring her to my clinic tomorrow, there is a lady doctor who can help her with the check-up.'

'What are you saying, Doctor sahib, is everything okay?' Salman asked, shocked.

'Yes! Yes! All okay, just a normal check-up,' the doctor replied, taking a small packet from his briefcase and handing it to Salman. 'I almost forgot, congratulations on your marriage *miyaa* (brother)!' The doctor smiled and walked off.

Salman was confused and looked at the box that read in English 'Deluxe Nirodh', with a man and a woman holding hands on a sunset background. He turned the box to read its explicit description of how to use a condom. Salman was bit embarrassed with the doctor's sudden choice of gift. He quickly gave fees to the doctor and showed him to the streets. Laughing, he casually threw the package into the bin across the street, where the municipality van was waiting to pick up the garbage. *As if I need that*, Salman thought. The government was determined to restrict new births, but Salman's family would never hear of it. He rushed to fetch the hakim, as he was still not convinced with the doctor and opted for his grandmother's choice.

Everyone back at home was surprised to see Salman return with a hakim. 'Is everything okay, Salman?' Salman's mother asked.

Salman signalled her to be quiet and ordered the hakim to check Shabana.

The hakim seemed pleasant and smiled at Shabana. 'Relax *beti*, I will be quick.'

Shabana nodded. '*Salam*,' she said to the hakim.

He took Shabana's hand to check her pulse, then checked her eyes and asked to show her tongue. 'Hmm ... Do you have pain in your abdomen?'

Shabana looked at the hakim with a blank face. 'No, hakim sahib.'

The hakim smiled and then turned to Salman's mother. '*Bibi*, can I ask your daughter some private questions?'

'Sure, Hakim sahib,' she replied.

'When was the last time you had your menstrual – as in, what is your menstrual cycle? Do you have cramps?'

Shabana felt very tired and uncomfortable with the question. 'Three weeks ago, and yes, Hakim sahib, I have cramps.'

'I see ... *beti*, you need rest. Some women tend to be very weak and tired after their cycle. Have plenty of rest and add a tablespoon of *tulsi* (basil leaves) to one cup of boiling water. Cover it and make sure you allow it to cool. Drink this every three hours to ease cramps.' The hakim looked at Salman's mother as well while giving his remedy to Shabana. He continued, 'During your menstrual cycle – now, get a pen and write this carefully, *beti*.'

Salman's mother signalled Shabana to remain seated as she went to fetch a pad with a pen. Handing the pad and pen to Shabana, she sat next to her daughter-in-law so she could see what and how she wrote, as Salman's mother had heard a lot about Shabana's education. She wanted to be proud of her, but in fact felt very jealous.

'Boil ginger for five minutes and cool it. Once it's cool, add ginger and honey – drink this three times a day during your menstrual cycle. I will come at the end of next month to see how you are doing.' The hakim smiled at Shabana when she noticed that she wrote in Urdu instead of Bengali. 'That's very impressive. These days all the Muslim women want to write Bengali.' The hakim bid his goodbyes to both Shabana and her mother-in-law.

'Now take rest, as tonight is a big night for both of you,' Salman's mother teased.

'*Mami*, I ...'

Shabana was interrupted by Salman's mother. 'Child, will you stop addressing me as your maternal aunt? Call me *Aami*.'

Shabana hesitated for a while, but then she agreed with a nod.

'Take rest, tonight is a big night – not only for you but for the family too. There will be a party in this house. All the neighbours are invited so put on your best smile,' Shabana's mother-in-law said in an animated tone.

The entire household was buzzing with preparation for the evening party. Shabana was resting on strict orders while the ladies of the house prepared biryani, fried eggplant, dhal and goat curry, as well as a favourite of any household parties among Bengalis, rich or poor: Ganguram's rossogulla. The soft spongy ball-shaped dumplings were made with cottage cheese and semolina dough, cooked in a light golden syrup made of sugar – one ball could easily win over anyone at a party. There is a saying in Bengali: 'The food can be average but the rasogulla has to be the best.'

Salman's household could afford these mouth-watering rossogullas, but they were not aiming to be extravagant or show-offs. For the Querishis, what mattered the most was their ego, their pride. As the groom's side of the family, their reputation mattered; they couldn't sell themselves short in front of the bride's family by feeding their guests some cheap stuff and be remembered for decades for it. Salman's parents wouldn't take that risk.

The biryani was slowly cooking away in a clay pot. Salman and Shabana's grandmother was adding coal to the oven and fanning away for new coals to catch fire. The outside air was hot and humid and it was even worse in the kitchen; the old lady was slowly cooking away in the heat along with the biryani. 'Salman, could you get the transistor in the kitchen, to at least hear something on the radio,' the grandmother yelled out.

'Coming, *nani jaan*.' Salman came running to the kitchen with the transistor and turned it on for his grandmother. '*Namaskar* (welcome) to Vividh Bharti – All India Radio – today's news.'

Salman's grandmother cursed under her breath. 'Salman *beta*, put some songs on, it's a wedding house – a celebration for my grandson and granddaughter,' she said, pulling Salman's cheek.

'Shh! *Nani jaan*, wait – the newsreader is saying something important here. *Abba*! Come here quickly,' Salman yelled at the top of his voice.

'…VK Krishna Menon, the great Indian nationalist and politician, died of heart attack in his residence on 6 Oct 1974, aged 78. It is a sad day for India. The flag at Rashtrapati Bhawan at the President's house will fly half-mast and also at all government offices. The government is planning a state funeral.'

'Oh Allah, another public holiday! How will I get those tailors to finish the orders – already so many holidays because of this government.' Salman cursed under his breath as he left the kitchen to get ready for the evening celebrations, leaving the transistor with his grandmother.

***

Lots of people brought gifts to the party. A tent was put up outside their house decorated with fairy lights and chairs facing a stage where Shabana and Salman sat in huge decorative chairs with gold painted on the carved wood. It was as if they were a king and queen. Jamshed and Mumtaz sat next to Shabana at one side and Salman's parents next to him.

Guests had to walk up the stairs to the stage to give the newlyweds gifts and blessings. The others sat on chairs or ate biryani and goat curry from the large table next to the stage. Salman's friends and other relatives were helping guests with the food. When the rossogulla came out there was almost a stampede. Music filled the air with the borrowed neighbourhood speakers and record player.

The evening was pleasant but the tension between Jamshed and Shabana was still there – not visible, but Mumtaz and Razia could sense it. The customary obligations finished at about 11.00 pm – one by one all the guests left. 'Ok, *Aami* will go now – take care of my daughter,' Mumtaz said, hugging her mother in tears.

Everyone exchanged hugs; when Shabana hugged Mumtaz she whispered, 'This was not right, *Aami*.'

Mumtaz looked at Shabana with sympathy in her eyes, but she had to maintain the family prestige. She said aloud, 'Now this is your house, your family. Look after them like you have looked after us.' She kissed Shabana on the forehead.

For the first time in two days Jamshed spoke to Shabana, looking directly into her eyes. 'If we hear any complaints, it won't be pleasant.' It was as though he was giving Shabana some sort of warning.

Seeing the situation becoming tense, Mumtaz's mother broke the ice. 'Come on everybody, let's not put so much pressure on her – she wasn't well this afternoon. Let them go and rest. It's their first night. Let us leave them alone,' she teased the newlyweds, pinching Salman's cheeks.

Shabana froze at the thought of spending her night with this man. She prayed in silence.

Once Salman and Shabana were both alone in Salman's room, Shabana wanted to run away; she caught the side of the bedsheet firmly in her fist at the sight of him walking towards her. 'I know this is awkward for both of us,' said Salman, 'you have been calling me brother but our families want this for us/want the best for us.'

He tried to reach out for Shabana's hands but she froze and shook her head, then slowly began to say, 'I need time, Salman.'

'What time? You are married to me and I am your husband, so why must I wait?' Salman asked in an angry tone. He grabbed her forcefully by her arms; in that tussle one of her glass bangles caught on the bedsheet.

'Salman! You are hurting me. Please not tonight.'

'It is our first night! Then which night?' Salman said impatiently.

'Can you please let go, you are hurting me and I want to go to the toilet,' Shabana requested.

'Sure, go and come back quickly.'

The moment he let go, she ran towards the door feeling relieved. A waiting audience seemed to have their ears pressed on the door; as Shabana swung the door open, her grandmother, Salman's mother and father came falling towards her.

Seeing Shabana's shocked face, her grandmother was again the first person to break the awkward silence. 'We were just checking if you and Salman were okay and if you needed something? Salman, you are looking after her, aren't you?'

'Yes, *nani jaan*, I am,' Salman replied, slightly embarrassed.

'*Nani*, can I go now to the toilet?' Shabana asked, embarrassed too.

'Yes! Yes, of course, please go. I will come with you; it's dark outside,' her grandmother insisted. Taking the torch in one hand, she took Shabana by the other hand and escorted her to the toilet that was outside in the courtyard. Shabana couldn't hold out any longer, running inside the toilet. She pressed her headscarf to her mouth to supress the noise of her weeping.

She was there for quite some time, agitating her grandmother. '*Beti*, is it done?'

Hearing her impatient grandmother, she quickly splashed some water over her face and quickly undid her salwar pants to squat on the toilet. 'Coming *Nani*,'

Shabana replied, but as she went to clean herself she noticed some bleeding. Quickly she did up her salwar pants and washed her hands. Shabana was relieved. 'Thank you Allah,' she whispered.

'What took you so long, *beti*?' This time her grandmother was concerned.

'*Nani*, I have some … vaginal bleeding.'

'Oh? Was Salman being rough on you?'

Shabana wanted to laugh at her concerned voice. 'No! No! he didn't do anything – I think this is because of my cramps.' Shabana was talkative now because of this sudden relief.

'Salman may have to wait then, and if you sleep with him he may want to … you know what I mean?'

'Yes *Nani*,' Shabana replied with her head hung in embarrassment.

'Don't be shy *Beti*, it's all nature. You will sleep with me tonight.' Shabana nodded to her grandmother's words.

Salman's mother approached and Shabana's grandmother beckoned her closer. 'Look, Shabana will be sleeping with me tonight, she's bleeding. Tell Salman's *abba* to take her to the lady doctor but I think call the hakim – that will be better.' Listening to her mother-in-law's concern, Salman's mother did as she was told.

When Shabana lay next to her grandmother she felt safe. *Hope Ted is okay*, Shabana thought.

***

It was 9.00 am when Shabana and Salman left for the lady doctor. She still felt weak. She realised she'd had nothing but a glass of water since last night. Shabana sat behind Salman on his scooter, careful not to touch him at all; the extra tyre of the scooter that Salman tied at the passenger seat came to her rescue for support.

There was no one waiting and because the compounder knew Salman, he made it easy for them to jump the queue. The lady doctor took Shabana into a small chamber and drew some curtains. She checked her abdomen and asked all the same questions as the other doctor.. 'Hmm! When did you last have sex after your period?' Shabana froze at her question and was thankful to God that Salman was not there. For a brief second she panicked and looked down at the floor. 'Don't be shy – I am a woman, so I can talk to you directly. Think about using contraceptives – not for you, but for your husband. The government is becoming strict – even with *Hum do, hamare do* ('We two, ours two'). In 1952 the government pleaded two or three children and stop, but now it might be even stricter. Do you understand what I am saying?'

Shabana looked at her blankly.

'One day, come with your husband so I can talk to both of you. For now I will tell your husband to bring you tomorrow to do some blood and urine tests. Fast for tomorrow. You can just have water.'

'You can do the tests, doctor jee. I haven't eaten anything,' Shabana replied.

'Not good, young girl – you need to look after yourself, otherwise no one will. Very well, I will ask the nurse to take your blood. Here is the cup – drink some water, fill up your bladder.' The doctor smiled at Shabana, handing her the cup.

***

'When will the report come?' Salman asked the nurse who handed him the receipt he needed in order to go pay the cashier.

'Come tomorrow around 4.00 pm to take the report.'

'Madam jee, can't that be done a little early?'

The nurse looked at Salman with a blank face. 'Yes – give 100 rupees and take it in the evening.'

Now Salman wanted to know more than anyone else why Shabana was bleeding – not because he was over-concerned, he just wanted to have sex with her. 'Yes! We'll pay the 100 rupees.'

Shabana was shocked, as it was quite a large amount for a silly report.

'Very well then! Come at 5.00 pm tonight and take the report – the cashier will give you a slip, take the slip and go to the pathology behind the gates,' the nurse replied.

***

It had been nearly two days. Ted hadn't heard or seen Shabana, nor had he seen Jamshed. Should he go to the kitchen to see if Jamshed was there? Would it be risky? *Why would I think it risky?* he thought. *Jamshed doesn't know.*

Finally he decided that he would not let fear dictate to him. He went downstairs towards the kitchen in an empty hallway. He could hear a few voices coming from there. Slowly he made his way into the kitchen. 'Lala jee, how are you?'

Lala jee smiled awkwardly. 'Ted sahib! You want something, some tea? I will bring to your room.'

'Thank you Lala jee, that won't be necessary. I just wanted to see if Jamshed was here?'

Lala jee nodded and before he could say something, Jamshed came walking into the kitchen from the pantry. 'Yes! You want to see me or do you … need anything?'

'No … I wanted to talk to you.' Ted gave a sincere look.

'Actually, I wanted to talk to you too. Lala jee, could you give us some space? And you too Chotu.' Once Lala jee and the dishwasher left, Jamshed said, 'Take a seat, babu sahib. Do you want water?'

'No,' Ted replied.

'Sit babu, make yourself comfortable,' Jamshed insisted. Ted still didn't know where this was going. 'Have you ever seen a cow slaughtered before?'

Ted thought that this was an odd question to ask. 'Yes, but—'

'I mean here in India,' Jamshed interrupted.

'No.' *Has he gone mad? What sort of questions are these?* Ted thought.

Picking up the butcher knife from the drawer, Jamshed raised it up to the tube-light to see it shine. Carefully with his index finger he rubbed the sharp blade. 'Sahib, you should see how we halal an animal. It dies a slow death as all the blood is drained from the body.'

'What are you trying to say, Jamshed? Just tell me as it is.' Ted feared the worst – he knew what was coming.

'You are intelligent, sahib. All I will say is that you should leave us and Shabana alone.' Jamshed folded his hands. 'We are common people, we don't mix with different races. We have …'

Ted cut him short. 'Listen to me Jamshed. I have no bad intentions towards Sha—'

Jamshed raised his hand signalled Ted to stop. 'That's it, sahib – no more of Shabana's name on your lips. You are lucky that you are under the Australian embassy – in another country's hand. If you were one of us … you wouldn't even know what would have hit you.'

'Are you threatening me, Jamshed?'

'No, sahib – I am warning you. No one knows about this … so if something happens to you, no one will know. Be careful.' Jamshed walked closer to Ted. 'She's married now, and I want you to respect this.' He turned his back and walked towards the kitchen door to fetch Lala jee and the dishwasher to resume work.

Before he could let the others in Ted stopped him, angry at the news of Shabana's marriage. Now what he suspected was confirmed. It had to be the same person who poisoned Mother's ears. He needed to find out. 'Jamshed, at least tell me how you knew about us.'

Jamshed smirked. 'Go ask Cathy, memsahib.'

Ted went white, feeling as if someone had pulled out the earth from beneath him.

'Shocked? So was I, sahib! I had that same look when I came to know you were taking advantage of my daughter. I knew about it some time ago but I wanted to see with my own eyes. You white people think it's just okay to have some fun.'

Ted stood there motionless before he gathered his wits to reply. 'No! Jamshed, that's not true – you cannot make assumptions about me like that.'

Before he could continue, Jamshed opened the door to let Lala jee in. 'Lala jee, sahib will be leaving now – could you make him some tea to be delivered to his room?'

'That won't be necessary Lala jee,' Ted replied and dashed out of the kitchen.

How could she? And why? Overcome with emotions, Ted hurried upstairs to Cathy's room for some answers. The anger inside that had brewed for Jamshed was now taking a new form – Ted was reluctant to accept what had happened in such a short period. *I couldn't even say goodbye to her. Why would someone be so mean and hurtful?*

'Who is it?' Cathy yelled in response to the banging on her door.

'It's me, Ted. Cathy, open up.'

Ted kept on banging the door until she came out. 'What's the matter with you, Ted?'

'You tell me, Cathy. What more can go wrong for me? You know what I mean, don't you? Is that what you were trying to tell me the other day at the dining hall?'

Cathy was shocked as she never thought Ted would find out. 'Could you just come in? We can talk this through.'

'There is nothing to talk about. How dare you, Cathy – how dare you? Did you call my mother for this? Did you?' Cathy froze, so he pressed on. 'Answer me, woman – did you?'

Ted screamed his lungs out, which made Cathy

jump out of her skin – she was shaking and her lips were trembling to speak the truth. 'Yes! Ted, I did – for us.' Ted frowned and she added, 'Ted, I did it for *you* – I couldn't bear the fact that you gave more time to a maid than me.' Cathy was almost in tears now.

Ted smashed his fist on the side of Cathy's door. His eyes were red, as if he was possessed. He was shaking with anger and he knew he had to calm himself down, otherwise someone might just get hurt. He closed his eyes, took a deep breath and said very softly, 'Did I ever give you any inclination that I liked you? Did I?'

'No ...' Cathy replied.

'Then why did you have to do all this – waste someone's life? You had no right to do anything for me. I hate you!' Ted walked away.

Cathy closed her eyes; covering her face with both hands, she fell down on the floor. She sobbed as she cried, 'What have I done?'

***

'Salman *beta*! Salman, where are you?' Shabana's grandmother called out from the courtyard.

'*Nani*, he has gone to the doctor to get the report. It's 4.30 now, he should be back soon,' Shabana yelled.

As Shabana was preparing tea for the family, she heard a big thud on the door. The thud grew to loud noises on the door. '*Aami*! Open the door!' People inside the house could hear Salman screaming.

'Coming!' Shabana rushed to open the door.

As soon as she opened the door, Salman pushed Shabana to the ground. He spat on her and screamed, '*Kutti kaheen ki* (bloody bitch)!' Seeing this, the grandmother, who was just few meters away from all that was happening, rushed towards Shabana and yelled for others to come out of the house.

'What is going on?' Salman's mother asked, rushing from her bedroom along with her husband.

'Ask her that question – the *sali kutti* is three weeks pregnant!'

Shabana was shocked. She wanted to disappear, or to run away to Ted and tell him the good news – but realising where she was, she instead wanted to bury herself.

'What are you saying Salman? Are you sure?' Salman's father asked as he joined them.

Salman looked at his father, swinging the reports in the air as he said, 'These reports don't lie.'

Everyone was shocked. 'Call the hakim – let us be sure,' the grandmother protested.

'Are you crazy, old woman? The doctor confirmed, what more do you need? Waste another hundred rupees on this *randi* (whore)?' Salman replied rudely.

'Wait, Salman *beta*, listen to your grandmother and call the hakim,' his mother insisted. Salman looked down on Shabana with spite as she sobbed quietly, covering her eyes with her scarf.

When the hakim arrived, Shabana's grandmother was firm. 'Go inside with him. You go with them,' she ordered both Shabana and Salman's mother.

'*Dekho Bibi* (Look ma'am), here I have brought a small pot of barley seed and wheat seed. Ask your daughter-in-law to urinate on both. If in three days it doesn't sprout, then she is not pregnant. If it comes to pass, that means she is. If the wheat sprouts then it's a girl, if the barley sprouts then it's a boy.'

Shabana's mother-in-law took the small pot. 'Aey! Take this and do what you have just been told – maybe the doctor was wrong.' She shoved it in Shabana's hand, looking at her with seething eyes.

'Bibi, if the doctor's report has come positive, then it's true – my test will confirm that too but it will basically confirm girl or boy. That will be exciting,' the hakim said innocently.

Listening to this, Shabana's mother-in-law wailed and buffeted everyone sitting outside in the courtyard 'Hai! *Dhoka* (betrayal)!'

'What happened?' Salman's father asked.

'Ask Hakim jee,' came the reply.

The hakim narrated everything and was quickly whisked out by Salman with two hundred rupees placed into his palm. The hakim looked at him in surprise. 'A hundred for your fees, and the other hundred is to keep your mouth shut.' The hakim nodded and left Salman's household to mourn.

'How dare Jamshed and Mumtaz betray us – and you, shameless woman, where did you go and grow this seed of sin?' Salman's mother screamed. 'You have spoiled my son's life, you witch!'

Salman's father ordered someone get Jamshed on the phone. When they spoke, the tone was not kind. 'Jamshed, come immediately. I am calling a *qadi* (Sharia magistrate) too. Bring the *meher* money with you.' Salman's father hung up.

***

Shabana's grandmother looked at Shabana with disgust, then walked away from her. Shabana just sat there motionless, not knowing what to do. *Should I call Ted and give him the good news that he is going to be a father?* Shabana thought. *What if he also decides to abandon me?* Shabana was contemplating all the possibilities when he heard Jamshed and Mumtaz's voices.

Salman's father and Salman ran towards the *qadi* and Jamshed. Mumtaz went towards the women who were waiting for her so they could all curse both Shabana and her. 'Take your whore daughter back with you – she has no place in this house of dignified people,' Salman's mother screamed at Mumtaz.

'*Aami*, what's happening? At least don't talk ill about your favourite granddaughter,' Mumtaz cried to her own mother for support.

'Mumtaz, Shabana is three weeks pregnant. Whose sin were you both trying to indulge us with?'

Mumtaz froze at those words. She turned to Shabana and with rage in her eyes, she started slapping and kicking her. 'Why didn't you die when you were born? Why did you make us see this day?'

'*Talaq! Talaq! Talaq!*' Salman screamed 'divorce' three times. He knew it would have been enough in front of his father, but he wanted to make it official in front of Jamshed and the *qadi*.

Salman's father folded his hands in front of Jamshed and Mumtaz. 'Please take your daughter with you and leave the *meher* money here. You have humiliated us enough. Please get out. Now!' Mumtaz's mother closed the door of her room.

Mumtaz dragged Shabana outside. Jamshed was quiet. Their heads hung in shame.

The moment they all reached home, Jamshed ordered Mumtaz to pack Shabana's things and he went to call for another taxi. Mumtaz, confused by all this, did what she was asked to do. Once he came back with the taxi he called for Razia. 'Razia, say goodbye to Appa – maybe this is the last you will see her here.'

Shabana was shocked at Jamshed's words. Razia and Mumtaz too were horrified. 'Where are you taking her, Jamshed?' Mumtaz yelled.

'Abba, please, listen to me. I will do whatever you will say, please don't take me from here! Aami, please talk to Abba.' Shabana was in tears. She yelled, 'Aami! Razia!' When Jamshed dragged her by her hair, everyone was watching at the servant's quarters. 'Lala jee! Please try to make Abba understand,' Shabana screamed.

James was crossing the servant's quarters to check on his laundry, as he hadn't seen Shyama Prasad with his shirts, and witnessed the whole spectacle between Jamshed and Shabana. He waited until Jamshed dragged Shabana to the taxi, and then ran outside to his waiting car and asked the driver to follow the taxi.

Inside the moving taxi, Shabana was crying profusely, gulping away every guilty sob. Jamshed held her hand tightly. When the taxi came to a halt Shabana was horrified to see where her father brought her. The taxi stood in Sonagachi, the red light district of Calcutta. 'Get out!' Jamshed yelled.

'*Abba*, no – please don't do this,' Shabana pleaded.

Jamshed sat motionless. He opened her door, kicked her out and told the taxi to drive away.

James waited until Jamshed's taxi passed by. He waited for another 10 minutes until he got out and took Shabana to his car. 'James sahib! Please help Ted,' Shabana pleaded to him, crying.

'I will! Let me take you first to a safe place from here,' James said to her.

Shabana narrated to James what happened on their way to James's Bengali friend's place. He held Shabana's hand tightly as she was sobbing away. 'It's okay, I am here. Tell me what's happened.'

***

'James! Good to see you. How have you been, young chap?'

'I'm very good Mr Basu,' James replied to a tall lean man with a French beard that was almost grey. 'Is Mrs Basu here?'

'Yes,' Mr Basu replied, 'but you look worried.'

'I am – not for me but for this young lady here.' James moved to the side for Mr Basu to see Shabana, who was hiding behind him. Mr Basu called out for his wife. 'Radhika! Look who's here! James, could you come here quickly please.'

'Mr Basu, this is Shabana: she's our caretaker's daughter, I just …' James hesitated for a moment, looking at Shabana, and then he began. 'I just rescued her from the doorsteps of a brothel.'

Mr Basu looked shocked as his wife joined them, confused by the entire situation. 'Is everything okay?' Mrs Basu asked.

'Yes, yes – could you please take the girl inside and give her some water and something to eat? I need to have a chat with James.'

Sensing that Mr Basu was worried, James quickly took him aside. 'Mr Basu, if you are worried that I have done something, then the answer is no. It has got something to do with someone in the embassy – I don't know what it is yet, but that's why I brought her here. Please let me talk to her first.'

There was a certain relief on Mr Basu's face from the reassurance.

Mrs Basu took Shabana inside and gave her some water and sweets to eat. Shabana quickly gulped the water. Seeing how thirsty she was, Mrs Basu gave her some cold water from the fridge. 'Have some sweets,' Mrs Basu offered.

'Thank you!' Shabana replied, taking a small rossogulla in her hand.

'Ahem!' Mr Basu cleared his voice as he entered the kitchen with James. 'Radhika, could you come to the living room here? I think James and Shabana need some privacy.'

Mrs Basu smiled at James and nodded at her husband as they left.

Once they were all alone, James pulled up a chair next to Shabana and asked, 'Are you okay now?'

Shabana nodded. 'Yes, James sahib.'

James smiled. 'Now tell me, what happened and why do you want me to help Ted?'

She looked away from him, slightly embarrassed, staring at the mosaic floor of the kitchen. 'James sahib, my father left me at a brothel because my husband just gave me *talaq* – he disowned me, like a divorce and … and …' She stammered and stopped. 'I am three weeks pregnant.'

'What has this got to do with Ted?'

Shabana looked up at James with tears in her eyes. 'Sahib … I think– no, I don't think, I am sure Ted is the father of this child.'

James froze, too shocked to say anything. To him, it seemed as if history was repeating again.

Shabana kneeled with her hands folded. 'Sahib, help Ted, your brother … *Abba* knows who the father is. He will kill him. You have to save him.'

James looked at Shabana with surprise. 'You know about me and Ted?'

'Yes! He was very distressed when he came to know about you – but I guess Ted is an amazing man who had the courage to ask for your forgiveness.' Shabana looked at him.

James picked Shabana up from the floor, smiled at her and said, 'Ted is a very lucky man. Stay here tonight – you will be safe here.'

'Sahib … Ted …?'

'He will be fine. He is at the office until 7.00 tonight. I will go now, it's close to here. No one can touch Ted. Your father works in a foreign territory.'

'You don't know my father,' Shabana replied worried.

'Relax! Mr and Mrs Basu will take care of you. I will try to bring him to you here, but I cannot promise.'

'Okay,' Shabana replied.

Just as James was heading towards the door, he stopped. 'Shabana, always listen to this.' He held his hand closely to his heart. 'It never lies.'

Shabana nodded.

When he told Mr and Mrs Basu what was happening, they were concerned too. 'James, this might get too political. An Indian girl, and on top of that she's Muslim, and a Western guy – as a good friend, I will advise you not to get into this mess. Help the girl, I am not stopping you – maybe get her out of Calcutta … or the young man from your office, who's in more danger than her.'

Mr Basu's words sent a shiver through James's spine. How could James tell him that the same man was his half-brother? 'You are correct – I'd better go and stop him from going to the living quarters.' He bid his goodbyes and couldn't thank Mr and Mrs Basu enough for all their help.

Once in the car, James handed the driver a bundle of hundred rupee notes. 'Five hundred rupees here to keep your mouth shut on Shabana to Jamshed. One word and I will make sure you are not only fired from the embassy, but also you don't get hired anywhere. More can come your way. You just have to keep your mouth shut.'

The driver couldn't be bothered with what James said; he just kept looking at the crisp hundred rupee notes. 'Sir, you have nothing to worry about,' the driver said, smiling.

Why wouldn't you, as it is almost your month's salary – bastard! James thought. On the way to his office, James was tense. But once he reached the office he was glad everything looked normal as he hustled his way inside.

'Ted, quick – in my office. Now!' James was not only glad to see him but had to make quick decisions, not only for him but also for the embassy's welfare. Once Ted was inside the office, James closed the door behind him and shut the blinds. 'Now listen to me carefully, Ted … you have to get the next flight out of Calcutta to Delhi. Leave everything now and come with me.'

'What's the matter?'

James didn't know how to break the news to Ted, but he had to. 'Ted, it's not safe for you to go back to the house. I have Shabana with me. I don't know how to say this.' James stopped.

'What are you saying, James? I'm confused. Why is Shabana with you?' There was an odd silence between them.

'Ted, sit down. What I am about to say to you … well, you might need to process this.' Obeying the order, Ted sat as James spoke. 'As you must know, Shabana got married.' Ted nodded. James continued. 'I rescued Shabana from the doorstep of a brothel today.'

'What? Wha … what are you saying?' Ted stammered.

'Jamshed dropped her there … you know why? Because not only did she get divorced by her husband, but … Ted, she's three weeks pregnant.'

Those words were enough for Ted to realise the intensity of the situation. Ted buried his face in his hands and whispered, 'What have I done?'

James walked closer to him. 'Are you sure … you are the father?'

Ted looked up. 'Yes! One hundred per cent, I can be sure of that.' Tears were building up in his eyes. 'Trust me, James, I had no intention – it just happened. I love her. She was the one who said to me that the past makes a lot of noise and I need to hear my own voice, and stand up for what I want.'

Those words were enough for James to trust Ted. 'I see! She is indeed a lovely girl and I can see how much you love her. Now listen to me carefully: I need you to go to the airport right now. Here is some money – board whatever flight is available to Delhi. I will speak to the chancellor there. This is totally out of protocol.'

'I can't, not right now. I have to see Shabana,' Ted protested, handing him back the money.

'Listen to me Ted, she's safe – please don't jeopardise that. Please. Write her a letter instead that I will give to her. Make it quick.'

'Just one last time – please. Brother,' Ted said.

'Are you punishing me, Ted? Killing me with those words – calling me brother?'

'I'm sorry for what happened to you and your mother – we both have the same blood and ... what our father couldn't do ... I want to acknowledge and give this baby a name.'

James was lost for words at first. 'You have no idea what this means to me.' He paused and smiled. 'Is there a saying ... maybe not ... that love is the biggest revenge? Is that what you are killing me with?'

'I think it is, James – I think it is.'

Both the brothers hugged each other. 'I will come with you to Shabana. Let's go now before I change my mind,' James said, rubbing his tears.

***

It was nearly half past seven when Ted arrived at Mr and Mrs Basu's residence. 'Come in James – oh! Hello, have we met before?' Mr Basu stared at James' new companion.

'This is Ted – the guy I told you about from the office.' Raising his eyebrows, James tried to be as discreet as possible.

'Oh … come in Ted, James. Please be seated.' Mr Basu realised he was forgetting his courtesy as the guests stood outside the door.

'Mr Basu, we are in a real hurry as Ted has to catch a flight … could … could he …' James stammered.

'Yes, of course. She's in the guest room,' Mr Basu replied.

'Come on Ted, let's be quick.' Ted followed James into the guest room. 'Shabana, look – I've kept my promise,' James said to Shabana, who had her back to them and was facing the city lights.

Sensing the intensity of the moment, James whispered in Ted's ear, 'Ten minutes – make it quick, please,' and walked out of the room.'

As soon as James left the room, Shabana ran to Ted. Smothering her with kisses softly, Ted whispered to Shabana, 'I am sorry I wasn't there for you.'

'It's okay *janemaan*, you are here now.' Shabana tried fighting her tears.

'Is it really true – I will be a father?'

'Yes! You will be a father and I will be there for the baby, for both of us.'

Taking Shabana's hands in his, Ted said, 'I want to

get married to you, bring you to Melbourne. We will have a home …' He stopped, realising that it was all going to be impossible; he was building her a dream based on false hope.

'Ted, look at me … I will always be yours, with or without a wedding. You have given me the most beautiful gift that will build hope – dreams for both of us.' Shabana thought she had her emotions in control but then she completely broke down. 'Ted, I need something more from you than this gift you have given me.'

'Anything, darling – whatever you want.'

Shabana looked at Ted closely. 'Promise?'

'Promise.'

'You will go to Melbourne – get married and completely forget about us. You have a life there. I don't want you to get into any more trouble, please … I already have you forever with me.'

Ted stood there speechless. 'No! No, I cannot do that – don't ask me this, please … don't!'

'Listen to me Ted, you can and you will.'

'Please Shabana!' Ted pleaded.

'*Janemaan*, we have already talked about it.' Shabana winked at Ted and continued. 'In the next life, no one can take me from you, or you from me.'

There was a moment of giggling between the two with tears in each other's eyes, interrupted by a knock on the door.

'Ted!' James called out.

'Just a second – coming,' Ted replied, grabbing Shabana in his arms. Silence filled the room; giving Shabana a gentle push, he walked out of the room, allowing the door to close with a thud. Shabana stood there motionless with her head hanging down. She jumped when the door thudded closed. She didn't turn back to stop Ted – not that it would weaken her, but she didn't want Ted to be weak.

***

On the way to the airport, Ted didn't speak. He looked outside at the moving world from the car, as if the city had sucked the life out of him. He withered inside, waiting to sacrifice the little hope that remained in him of surviving without Shabana and his unborn child. He would never see Shabana again. *How is that possible?* Ted thought over and over in his head.

'Ted – let's go mate,' James said softly to Ted as the car halted in front of Dum Dum International Airport. The tension was palpable.

James paid for his ticket. Ted had nothing with him – James shoved money into Ted's pocket. 'I will arrange everything from here to be sent to Delhi.' James hugged Ted. 'Come on, mate, time to go. Look after yourself.'

Ted shrugged and walked towards the security checkpoint.

James stood there for a long time until Ted vanished into the crowd in front. That was the last day James saw Ted: in Calcutta on 9 October 1974.

25 June 1975

T HE TELEVISION at the Visa office showed things in full swing. The president of India, Fakhruddin Ali Ahmed, officially declared India to be in a state of emergency because of the prevailing 'internal disturbance', effective indefinitely from 25 June 1975.

'Okay, boys,' James addressed his team, 'you are all going home early today, though – we don't know if there'll be any incidents. We have extra security ...'

'James, there's a private call for you on line three,' a colleague yelled out.

'Transfer it into my office,' James yelled back. 'Okay! Everything is going to shut early – hope you all make it to dinner at least.' James laughed along with others.

On the phone: 'Hello James, Basu here ... we are taking Shabana to the emergency now.'

'I will be on my way soon. Which hospital again?'
James asked anxiously.

'PG Hospital.'

James hung up quickly and ran for the car outside.

The traffic was horrendous near Park Street; everything was at a standstill. James was stuck there for almost an hour. It took another 45 minutes to reach St Paul's Cathedral – the hospital was just another 15 minutes away. To James it seemed forever. The quick 15 minutes to the hospital turned to 30 minutes in the stop-and-start traffic jam.

Once he reached the hospital, he asked the driver to go back and end his duty for the day too. 'My friend will drop me off.'

'Are you sure, sahib? I can wait.'

'Go,' James ordered and ran inside.

He was making his way to the reception when he saw Mr Basu. 'Basu, I am here.'

'James, they're just shifting Shabana to the room. It's a girl.'

James waited to catch his breath. 'Basu, I am an uncle now!' Saying it aloud, he sat down in tears.

'I can understand how you feel … I wish the father was here too,' Mr Basu said softly. James had earlier taken Mr Basu into his confidence and confessed the truth between himself and Ted. It was hard for James – but then, what explanation could he have given for doing so much for two strangers?

'Go inside – go and meet her,' Mr Basu said, pointing at one of the rooms.

James ran inside and saw a frail Shabana lying in a bed, holding the baby wrapped in cloth. 'Congratulations! You're the father?' The nurse asked.

'No, the uncle,' James replied.

'You must see how beautiful she is. Looks like a doll,' said the nurse.

Shabana smiled at James. 'There you go, Uncle James: your niece,' she said softly.

He looked at the tiny body wrapped in hospital sheets in Shabana's arms, her eyes twinkling. Her face was as white as paper could be. 'Oh my god, she is beautiful,' said James.

'I know – she looks like Ted. Isn't it funny? No one can even say it's my baby.'

'Things can change, Shabana … she's just an infant,' James protested.

'No, I know she will be like Ted.' Shabana smiled. 'Oh! Talking of Ted, I've read his letter. He is well and is quite busy with his father's political career. He could be the next big thing.'

James couldn't stop playing with his niece. Shabana felt sad that Ted was not there with her and his daughter. She looked at her baby girl and James – for a moment she wanted to cry at this injustice. *Three of us left for love and without love. What an irony,* Shabana thought.

Changing her thoughts, she looked at James, who couldn't stop playing with the baby girl. 'How is *Abba*?'

James focused on playing with his niece, trying to avoid the question altogether.

*****

From the night Ted left, Jamshed and James had had their tensions and differences. The morning after Ted left for Delhi, Jamshed was ordered to pack Ted's room. Ted's safety was still James's foremost priority. That same night, Jamshed knocked on James's room. 'Who is it?' James asked.

'Jamshed, sahib.'

'Come in,' James replied, worried.

'Sahib, I have a request to make. I know why Ted sahib left suddenly and why also this … bureaucratic crap is all around me,' Jamshed said, looking at James helplessly.

'What do you mean?' James pretended as if he knew nothing.

'Sahib, we both know what has happened and it's best not to pretend. If it's Delhi – Calcutta – Bombay. It won't take much at all to find him.'

'What is that supposed to mean, Jamshed?' James asked.

'The poor always gets injustice, sahib – I lost my own daughter in this,' Jamshed said with a hint of sadness in his voice.

'I am sorry to hear that, Jamshed, but there is nothing I can do.' James wanted to sound empathetic but couldn't afford to give even one hint about Shabana. Jamshed was very intelligent.

Jamshed folded his hands in front of James. 'Sahib, please help me … please tell me as a father what I should do.'

'I wish I could, but I cannot advise you on that.' Walking Jamshed to the door James bade him goodnight. James sensed something was not quite right. *Was this a threat?* James thought.

The next morning, he didn't take any risks and called Ted to advise him of the danger that was still imminent. Ted knew what Jamshed was capable of

– he thought of the conversation between Jamshed and himself in the kitchen. 'You need to get back to Melbourne ASAP,' James pleaded with Ted. 'You have to talk to the chancellor and tell him the truth. I will be honest … you could be fired.'

'I will resign,' Ted replied. 'I cannot put Shabana's and the baby's lives at risk.'

Within a few weeks of that conversation, Ted left for Melbourne. After that, James tried to keep himself busy at work and avoided Jamshed.

***

'He is fine … don't worry about Jamshed. You have enough to worry about now,' James replied to Shabana.

Shabana nodded, taking the baby from James.

'What will you name her?' James asked, changing the topic.

Shabana looked at the baby girl for a long time and then replied, 'Rosemary.'

'Why, that's a mighty English name,' James said laughing.

'It is how I want to see Ted in her,' Shabana said with tears in her eyes.

'I know – I can understand,' James said, squeezing her shoulders. 'I will come tomorrow – better to leave early tonight. Emergency has been declared. You need rest too.' He gave both Rosemary and her mother a kiss on their forehead.

***

A month later, Shabana travelled to Khidirpur Road to answer an ad in the newspaper: 'Maid wanted at Karma Orphanage.' She wanted to get away from everything. From James, Ted and *Abba,* her family and everything connected with Ted. She now had his love to look after. *Am I being selfish? How can I repay James?* Shabana thought.

One morning she took baby Rosemary in her arms and walked out of Mr and Mrs Basu's residence. She left a note thanking them for everything and declaring it was now time for her to move away from the past and look after the present, for the future.

30 August 2017, 8.00 am

The Letter

I DIDN'T WANT to see Mum today; something didn't fit. Looking at Michael, I felt somewhat calm. I wanted to spend the rest of my life with him and our baby. I quietly kissed Michael's lips. *Eeek! He's moving.*

'Rosemary, let me sleep, darling. I have another night shift. Go and get dressed, I'll drop you off at work,' Michael murmured.

'What will I do with you, Michael? You are forgetting I have tea with Mum in the hospital today. I have the day free. Please drop me off on your way to work.' I looked at my watch; I had better cook some breakfast for Michael. The hustle and bustle of Brunswick Street was also waking up with Michael; it was always a marvel to see him cursing when I opened the window to the bedroom, the cold spring air waking him up.

The aroma of pancakes soon filled the air and Michael got up. 'Coffee?' I asked.

'That would be great,' Michael replied, winking at me. 'How's our baby girl doing?'

Michael knew I wanted a boy, but I guessed I would be happy with either.

'Why does Dorothy want to see you today?' he added.

'I wish I knew,' I said, 'but honestly, I don't know. The mother-daughter catch-up I guess.'

'Will you tell her the news of you expecting our child?'

I looked at Michael, who was as excited as I was. 'Of course!' I replied. 'I love you Michael.' I didn't know why I said that, but I had the urgency to tell him how much I loved him and I could feel tears rolling from my eyes.

'Baby! What's wrong?' Michael ran towards me, taking me in his arms.

'I guess it's hormones,' I replied.

'I love you, my darling.' Michael kissed me, patting my back. I felt as if I didn't tell Michael enough – of how much I loved him and appreciated him, and how lucky I felt to carry his child.

***

'Come on, let's get going – it's 4.15 already and you know how punctual Dorothy is with dinner.' Michael looked at me with his big brown eyes. 'Chop chop!'

'I'm coming, you know how much of an effort I have to make to see Mum,' I yelled out.

Once inside the car I felt calm. 'Okay, don't forget to remind her that she has to reply to the bowling club for the fundraiser,' said Michael.

'Thanks! I almost forgot,' I replied. As we approached the hospital, I suddenly felt anxious. I didn't want to go. My legs felt heavy.

'What's wrong, babe?' Michael asked.

'Nothing,' I replied. I kissed Michael goodbye and walked into the hospital.

'Hello, Mother!' I kissed Dorothy on her forehead. 'How are you feeling?'

'I am great. Look what I ordered – some Chinese food from your favourite shop,' Dorothy replied.

'Yum, sounds like a very good plan,' I replied. 'Any special occasion?'

'I have something to give you … a very special something that I had been saving for almost thirty-two years,' Dorothy said.

'I, too, want to tell you something,' I said with a smile. 'You first.'

Dorothy seemed to be in a happy mood. 'Let's eat first,' she requested.

I warmed the food and we treated ourselves to some amazing Chinese broccoli, fried rice and Mongolian beef. We were almost done with our dinner when Dorothy requested I take an envelope from her drawer. I handed her a glass of water while taking her plate from her, then went to the drawer to take the envelope out, finding a letter inside.

I read the letter quietly, digesting every word. Slowly getting a grip on myself, I looked at Dorothy. 'Is this some kind of joke?' I asked, annoyed with the letter.

'Every word I have written is true and I need to be honest with you. I think I have tortured you enough.' I could hear her crying.

'Why now? What do you want me to do? I find out today that my mother is actually my grandmother and my ayah my mother, who was rescued by my father's half-brother,' I yelled at her.

'Calm down dear! I will explain—'

'Calm down? You are telling me to calm down. What kind of fuck-up is this?' I couldn't control my language today.

'Shabana was waiting for your father after he was sent by James to Delhi to escape Jamshed – but I got to Shabana before Ted did. She came back from the church converted as a Catholic with a different name, but Cathy told me everything – she saw Shabana in the church. That's how I got to her.' Dorothy hesitated to tell the rest but continued. 'Your father did come back for her, but she left to work as an ayah until you were born. She followed you to Karma.' Dorothy sipped her water.

The image of Karma flashed before me, of Anita and Shabana. 'I hate you, Dorothy. I hate you for giving me this *awesome* gift of honesty.' I didn't know what else to say. All my life I'd looked for my identity and she'd stolen my childhood from me – how could she? I picked up my bag, rubbing my tears. I looked at Dorothy one last time.

'You will heal, my dear. Give yourself time, this will pass for us both,' Dorothy said to me.

'Seriously, is it that easy for you to say? I hate you, Dorothy Smith, for stealing my identity.' I stormed away without saying my final goodbye to her.

30 August 2017, 8:30 pm

Rosemary's Apartment

T HE GHOSTS OF THE PAST always make noise – as they were doing for me, forty-two years after my birth to Shabana and Ted. Was I at peace now, knowing the truth? I didn't know, but I tried to imagine explaining it all to my unborn daughter – to whom I would give all my love – what would I tell her if she asked where I came from? How could I tell her that her mother's identity had been concealed by her own family?

Could I forgive Dorothy? Never – nor could I forgive anyone who had been involved in my making.

I couldn't say all this to my unborn child. No! I couldn't be like Shabana and leave everything behind to be a martyr.

I picked up the sharpest knife from the kitchen, looking at how it shone under the kitchen light. How would it feel to kill Dorothy? At the same time, the thought of slitting my wrists enters my mind. *What is the colour of blood?* My eyes, foggy and obscured with tears, fixed onto two images in a photograph.

I heard someone open the door. 'Honey, I'm home,' Michael called out.

'Michael!' I called out. 'Hel … help!' I tried to call out for him but couldn't, my legs were heavy – losing my balance, I fell to the ground and whispered, 'Vengeance, it shall be now.'

31 August 2017, 8.30 am

EIGHTY-TWO-YEAR-OLD Dorothy Smith was eating her breakfast when she heard a knock at the door of her hospital room. 'Come in!' She placed her toast down and reached for her glasses near the drawer. 'Michael! What brings you at this hour?'

'I am here about Rosemary … she's been in the Emergency. She is okay now, out of danger.'

'What happened?' Dorothy asked in shock.

'You tell me. She was here yesterday. What is with this letter and photo?' Michael handed Dorothy the letter and the photograph. She looked at her own handwriting, took off her glasses and looked outside the window.

The letter read:

My dearest Rosemary,

You have always known me to be straightforward and honest. Today, when death is slowly creeping onto my side, I only fear losing you – and despite that fear I write this letter to you.

I don't have the courage to face you with the truth but this letter shall explain your past. With this letter, I want to make peace with the past and with you.

What I am about to tell you is something you will not like, but I hope you can forgive me. I wanted to give you this on your 40th birthday. But I waited a little while longer – now I know it's time. I have no appropriate gift to give you but the truth.

Since I rescued you from the orphanage back in 1987, you have grown to know me as your mother and I will always remain that. The truth is, Rosemary, that you are my own flesh and blood. I am your grandmother.

Your father, my son, was a diplomat stationed by the foreign office there. There he met your mother, Shabana, who was a maid in the foreign office.

Things were very different in the 70s. Your grandfather was standing election for local MP at that time and to have a scandal like this, even from abroad, would forever doom his political career. I, too, refused to accept and wanted nothing to do with you. I rushed overseas to meet your father and settle the issue. But I think your father and my stepson James decided to take matters into their own hands. I didn't know your mother too well but I can say this much: she was a proud woman.

She really loved your father and kept you. I am thankful to God and her for keeping you alive.

Shabana asked Ted not to meet her anymore, and your father kept his promise. True love never dies – only vanity does. Your father never got married.

After a few years, there was an article in the paper's World section. The article was about a girl, aged five, being brought up in an orphanage overseas. The interview of the matron Anita mentioned how you were found in a cot outside the door of the orphanage. She tried to find the true parents but failed. Your father saw a photograph of you, with your blue eyes – a striking resemblance to him when he was a child.

He went overseas and located your mother, who was your ayah – Shabana. She was stubborn and such was her love for you that she didn't want to return with him.

Your father suffered a heart attack on his return flight to us. With him we found a letter that detailed everything; he begged us to rescue you both. That was his last wish.

I travelled overseas a few years later to take custody of you both. Shabana saw me and knew instantly she would lose you forever. I heard the news of her accident the very day I came to fetch both of you. But I suspect she committed suicide. You see, I told her about your father when she came to meet me the same morning. I begged for her forgiveness and that she come with us. She refused but was happy that I accepted you. I was shocked when I learned about her accident. Her secret died with her in that accident, and I thought that was best for the time being.

I took you with me as a Good Samaritan rescuing a child from a foreign shore, giving you a comfortable home. We always made sure no one would talk about your father around the house. Your grandfather still couldn't accept you and he hated your father. I hid all your father's photographs and memories and locked them away in the attic. For me it was just an excuse to hide the truth from you for thirty years. I couldn't afford to risk anything further – the men in this family damaged my soul and I didn't know if I would recover from it.

You know when you moved away from our house to be with Michael, you saw a photograph of a young man in my bedroom. I lied to you, claiming it was a distant cousin. He was my son, your father, and when I was diagnosed with cancer, this photograph gave me the strength to tell you the truth. With his courage, I am able to write to you today.

I beg for your forgiveness; I know I have been wrong. There was no room for an outcast in the 70s and people were very unforgiving, my child. I hope you understand.

Your life with Michael will start soon and I hope this truth will set both of us free for a new beginning.

Please forgive me and release me from this debt.

Yours sincerely,

Grandmother Dorothy

'You had no right to play with her life and mine,' snapped Michael. 'You lost your son over thirty years ago but today … what were you thinking? Dorothy, she is two months pregnant – she was so excited to tell you yesterday. What did you get out of this? You could have left everything as it was.' He walked closer to Dorothy and said softly, 'Are you at peace now?'

Michael turned away and slammed the door behind him.

Dorothy looked at the photograph of her son and Shabana; tears were unstoppable. She closed her eyes and went into a deep sleep. When the nurse came to get her for her morning walk, she did not wake up.

Dorothy was declared dead at eleven in the morning on the 31st of August, 2017. She died unforgiven.

Acknowledgements

I THANK ROSALIE HAM for correcting my first-ever story written in those classes at RMIT. The birth of *Rosemary's Retribution* began in those classes in 2007.

Aisling, I thank you for taking my story to the world and the amazing bond that we share – it's not only a pleasure to work with you but you are my amazing pocket-rocket Irish chick. Thank you so much. I can write a million stories but they wouldn't be read if it wasn't for you.

A big thank you to my editor Beau for shaking up the writer in me, nudging those emotions onto the paper and sometimes disagreeing with me very discreetly. For that I will always be thankful. I salute you.

I also want to take this opportunity to thank Les who has been a huge influence in shaping my writing for the last few years, and for his incredible willingness to bring out the best in me and to guide me through. You are the best.

Also to the most beautiful couple – Kev and Blaise. Kev, for not only walking with me through those difficult paths and memories of Delhi, but I guess also for finding that brother in you. I will always cherish our walk at the Lotus Temple. Blaise, for your continued support from that day in September to today – you have been my rock.

A big thank you to Georgina Hanna and Tanya Poupard for taking my story to the Royal Melbourne Hospital Allied Health Department – you girls are like diamonds.

Also a big thank you to all my friends who have supported me through all the crises – your support on those dark days was enormous.

Lastly, I thank this beautiful universe as I put my everything out to you – my writing, my love for me, my peace, myself. In return, you gave back everything with a bonus – the love of my family, my mother and my sister. Thank you !

About the Author

NANDITA CHAKRABORTY was born in Kolkatta, India in 1975 in a small conservative family which has always been associated with the arts. Her father won many accolades in Indian cinema; his film *In Search of Famine* was the first Indian film in a regional language to win the Silver Bear at the Berlin Film Festival in 1980. The whole house would be surrounded by action and glamour, with well known artists sparking Nandita's creative mind at the dinner table or at her mother's dressing table.

Along with her siblings, she was sent out to boarding school at the age of seven in the hills of Meghalaya, India. A few years down the track the family settled in New Delhi, where she attended Sri Venketeswara University in New Delhi to study political science by day – and at night she would attend her fashion and visual merchandising school.

In her third year in college, she went on to pursue a Diploma in Visual Merchandising, leaving behind her career in Political Science. She began to work with a well known designer in India, finding fame and fortune in that path – but it still did not leave her creatively satisfied. Lying awake in her bedroom, she would often write poetry to herself. Secretly she wrote short stories about her adventures in her designing career. Often these would either land in the dustbin or make their way into the hands of junk dealers making paperbacks for grocery shopping.

In 2000 she came to Melbourne where she started her own fashion boutique with her partner. It was not until after a difficult divorce that she began searching for something that would define her purpose in life. She found solace in writing again.

In 2008 she joined RMIT to do a short course in creative fiction writing. Attending several book clubs, writing seminars and participating in many writing competitions, she met with some remarkable writers. Later she began to write short stories for the local newspaper and magazine in Melbourne.

Her first book, which she began writing in 2010, was self-published in 2013. It's an autobiography called *Missing Peace: Love, Life & Me*, detailing her quest for peace, love and life.

In 2011, she met with an accident while rock climbing, falling 40 metres and acquiring a traumatic brain injury. After several months in rehab she continued working but in 2016 she was back in rehab. She has a disability which cannot be seen, also known as a blind disability, and suffers from vestibular pain in her head with permanent cognitive issues, resulting in fatigue. She's not only fighting her disability but also depression and anxiety.

Currently she's a volunteer as a consumer representative at the Royal Melbourne Hospital Allied Health NDIS governance committee.

Nandita is also the author of 2017's *Meera Rising*, a modern re-telling of the Mirabai fable.

Meera Rising

WHEN MEERA SEN comes to the city of Melbourne to become a microbiologist, all she has with her are the traditional values of her culture and the idol of lord Krishna given to her by her uncle.

When Meera meets Brian for the first time, she hates him – but Brian falls in love with her instantly. Even as he desires her, Brian, consumed with his own insecurities, risks driving her away instead.

Living in Australia, and then returning to her homeland to reconnect with her family and the obligations waiting for her, will leave Meera no stranger to heartbreak. And when it seems this world has failed her, will Meera find fulfilment elsewhere?

Inspired by the life of Mirabai, our Meera's been bestowed with not one but with two lovers who fight to win her love: a mortal Brian seeks to rescue Meera and take her back to the temporal world, whilst the immortal Krishna invites Meera to his permanent world.

Meera Rising is the unforgettable story of an ordinary woman who dares to become an immortal saint – the extraordinary 'modern Mirabai'.